The Moon-Calves
AND OTHER TALES FROM THE PULPS

The Moon-Calves
AND OTHER TALES FROM THE PULPS

John D. Swain

WILDSIDE PRESS

THE MOON-CALVES AND OTHER TALES FROM THE PULPS

An original publication of Wildside Press, LLC.
Copyright © 2004 by Wildside Press, LLC.
All rights reserved.

For more information, contact:
www.wildsidepress.com.

Contents

Lucifer. 7

The Affair at Baker's Bluff. 16

The Old Man of the Sea 25

The Goat of Dolores Valdez 34

The Getaway 45

The Fist in Pacifist 61

The Cipher 72

Robbing the Roost 87

The Fascination of Guilt 98

Nearly a Football Team 111

Desperate Remedies 133

Hunger 151

The Moon-Calves 155

Lucifer

THE NOTORIOUS Remsen Case was table talk a year or so ago, although a few today could quote the details offhand. Because of it, half a dozen men were discussing psychic trivialities, in a more or less desultory way. Bliven, the psychoanalyst, was speaking.

"It all hinges on a tendency which is perhaps best expressed in such old saws as: 'Drowning men clutch at straws,' 'Any port in a storm,' or, 'A gambling chance.'

"When men have exhausted science and religion, they turn to mediums, and crystal-gazers, and clairvoyants, and patent medicines. I knew an intelligent pharmacist who was dying of a malignant disease. Operated on three times. Specialists had given him up. Then he began to take the nostrums and cure-alls on his own shelves, although he knew perfectly well what they contained — or could easily enough have found out. Consulted a lot of herb doctors, and long-haired Indian healers, and advertising specialists."

"And, of course, without result," commented the little English doctor.

"I wouldn't say that," said Bliven. "It kept alive the forlorn spark of hope in his soul. Better than merely folding his hands and waiting for the inevitable! He was just starting in with a miraculous Brazilian root, when he snuffed out. On the whole, he lived happier, and quite possibly longer, because of all the fake remedies and doctors he spent so much money on. It's all in your own mind, you know. Nothing else counts much."

"All fakes, including the records of the P.S.R.," nodded Holmes, who lectured on experimental psychology.

The little doctor shook his head depreciatingly.

"I shouldn't go as far as that, really," he objected, "because, every now and then, in the midst of their conscious faking, as you call it, with

7

the marked cards and prepared slates, the hidden magnets and invisible wires and all, these mediums and pseudo-magicians come up against something that utterly baffles them. I have talked with a well-known prestidigitator who has a standing bet of a hundred guineas that he can duplicate the manifestations of any medium; and yet he states that every now and then he finds himself utterly baffled. He can fake the thing cleverly, you understand; but he cannot fathom the unknown forces back of it all. It is dangerous ground. It is sometimes blasphemy! It is blundering in where angels fear to tread."

"Piffle!" snorted Bliven. "The subconscious mind explains it all; and we have only skirted the edge of our subject. When we have mastered it, we shall do thing right in the laboratory that will put every astrologer and palmist and tea-ground prophet out of business."

Nobody seemed to have anything to answer, and the psychoanalyst turned to the little doctor.

"You know this, Royce," he asserted, a bit defiantly.

"I don't pretend to follow you new-era chaps as closely as I ought; but I recall an incident in my early practice that is not explicable in the present-day stage of your science, as I understand it."

Bliven grunted.

"Well — shoot!" he said, "Of course, we can't check up your facts, but if you were an accurate observer, we may be able to offer a plausible theory, at least."

Royce flushed at his brusque way of putting it, but took no offence. Everyone makes allowances for Bliven, who is a good fellow, but crudely sure of himself, and a slave to his hobby.

"It happened a long, long time ago," began Royce, "when I was an interne in a London hospital. If you know anything about our hospitals, you will understand that they are about the last places on earth for anything bizarre to occur in. Everything is frightfully ethical, and prosy, and red-tapey — far more so than in institutions over here, better as these are in many ways.

"But almost anything can happen in London, and does. You love to point to New York as the typical Cosmopolis — because it has a larger Italian population than has Rome, a larger German than Berlin, a Jewish than Jerusalem, and so forth. Well, London has all this, and more. It has nuclei of Afghans, and Turkomans, and Arabs; it has neighborhoods where conversation is carried on in no known tongue. It even has a Synagogue of Negro Jews — dating certainly from the Plantagenet dynasty, and probably earlier.

"Myriads spend all their lives in London, and die knowing nothing about it. Sir Walter Besant devoted twenty years to the collecting of data for his history of the city, and confessed that he had only a smattering of his subject. Men learn some one of its hundred phases passing well; Scotland Yard agents, buyers of old pewter or black-letter books, tea importers, hotel keepers, solicitors, clubmen; but outside of their own little broods the eternal fog, hiding the real London in its sticky, yellow embrace. I was born there, attended its University, practiced for a couple of years in Whitechapel, and migrated to the fashionable Westminster district; but I visit the city as a stranger.

"So, if anything mysterious were to happen anywhere, it might well be in London; although as I have said, one would hardly look for it in one of our solid, dull, intensely prosaic hospitals.

"Watts-Bedloe was the big man in my day. You will find his works in your medical libraries, Bliven; though I dare say he has been thrust aside by the onmarch of science. Osteopathy owes a deal to him, I think; and I know that Doctor Lorenz, the great orthopedist of today, freely acknowledges his own debt.

"There was brought to us one day a peculiarly distressing case; the only child of Sir William Hutchinson, a widower, whose hopes had almost idolatrously centered in this boy, who was a cripple. You would have to be British to understand just how Sir William felt. He was a keen sportsman; played all outdoor games superlatively well, rode to hounds over his own fields, shot tigers from an elephant's back in India, and on foot in Africa, rented a salmon stream in Norway, captained the All-English polo team for years, sailed his own yacht, bred his own hunters, had climbed all the more difficult Swiss peaks, and was the first amateur to operate a biplane.

"So that to natural parental grief was added the bitter downfall of all the plans he had for this boy; instructing him in the fine art of fly-casting, straight shooting, hard riding, and all that sort of thing. Instead of a companion who could take up the life of his advancing years were forcing him to relinquish, in a measure, he had a hopeless cripple to carry on, and end his line.

"He was a dear, patient little lad, with the most beautiful head, and great, intelligent eyes; but his wretched little body was enough to wring your heart. Twisted, warped, shriveled — and far beyond the skill of Watts-Bedloe himself, who had been Sir William's last resort. When he sadly confessed that there was nothing he could do, that science and skillful nursing might add a few years to the mere existence of the little martyr, you will understand that his father came to that pass which you, Bliven, have illustrated in citing the case of the pharmacist. He was, in short, ready to try anything: to turn to quacks, necromancers, to Satan himself, if his son might be made whole!

"Oh, naturally he had sought the aid of religion. Noted clergy of his own faith had anointed the brave eyes, the patient lips, the crooked limbs, and prayed that God might work a miracle. But none was vouch-safed. I haven't the least idea who it was that suggested the to Luci-ferians to Sir William."

"Luciferians? Devil worshipers?" interrupted Holmes. "Were there any of them in your time?"

"There are plenty of them today; but it is the most secret sect in the world. Huysmand in La-Bas has told us as much as has anyone; and you know perfectly well, or should, that all priests who believe in the Real Presence, take the utmost care that the sacred wafer does not pass into irresponsible hands. Many will not even place it on the communicant's palm; but only in his mouth. For the stolen Host is essential to the cele-bration of the infamous Black Mass which forms the chief ceremony of the Luciferian ritual. And every year a number of thefts, or attempted thefts, from the tabernaculum, are reported in the press.

"Now the theory of this strange sect is not without a certain distorted rationality. They argue that Lucifer's Star of the Morning, was cast out of Heaven after a great battle, in which he was defected to be sure, but not destroyed, nor even crippled. Today, after centuries of missionary zeal, Christianity has gathered only a tithe of the people into its fold; the great majority is, and always has been, outside. The wicked flourish, often the righteous stumble; and at the last great battle of Armageddon, the Luciferians believe that their champion will finally triumph.

"Meanwhile, and in almost impenetrable secrecy, they practice their infamous rites and serve the devil, foregathering preferably in some abandoned church, which has an altar, and above it a crucifix, which they reverse. It is believed that they number hundreds of thousands, and flourish in every quarter of the world; and it is presumed that they employ grips and passwords. But amid so much that is conjecture, this fact stands clear: the cult of Lucifer does exist, and has from time immemorial.

"I never had the least idea who suggested them to Sir William. May have been some friend who was a secret devotee, and wished to make a proselyte. Nay have been an idle word overheard in a club — or penny bus. The point is, he did hear, discovered that an occult power was claimed by their unholy priests, was ready to mortgage his estate or sell his soul for this little chap, and somehow got in touch with them.

"The fact that he managed it, that he browbeat Watts-Bedloe into permitting one of the fraternity to enter the hospital at all, is the best example I an give of his despairing persistence. At that, the physician agreed only upon certain seemingly prohibitive conditions. The fellow was not to touch the little patient, nor even to draw near his bed. He was not to speak to him, or seek to hold his gaze. No phony hypnotism, or anything like that.

"Watts-Bedloe, I think, framed the conditions in the confident hope that they would end negotiations; and he was profoundly disgusted when he learned that the Luciferian, though apathetic, was not in the least deterred by the hardness of the terms. It appeared that he had not been at all willing to come under any circumstances; that he tried persistently to learn how Sir William had heard of him, and his address, and that he had refused remuneration of any sort. Altogether, a new breed of fakir, you see!

"There were five of us in the room at the time appointed, besides the little patient, who was sleeping peacefully. Fact is, Watts-Bedloe had taken the precaution of administering a sleeping draught, in order that the quack might not in any possible way work upon his nervous system. Watts-Bedloe was standing by the cot, his sandy hair rumpled, his stiff moustache bristling, for all the world like an Airdale terrier on guard. The father was there, of course; and the head nurse, and a powerful and taciturn orderly. You can see that there wasn't much chance of the devil-man pulling off anything untoward!

"When, precisely on the moment, the door opened and he stood before us, I suffered as great a shock of surprise as ever in my life; and a rapid glance at my companions' faces showed me that their amazement equaled mine. I don't know just what type we had visualized — whether a white-bearded mystic clad in a long cloak with a peaked hat bearing cabalistic symbols, or a pale, sinister and debonair man of the world, such as George Arliss has given us, or what not; but certainly not the utterly insignificant creature who bowed awkwardly, and stood twirling a bowler hat in his hands as the door closed behind him.

"He was a little, plump, bald man of middle age, looking for all the world like an unsuccessful greengrocer, or a dealer in butter and cheese in a small way. Although the day was cool, with a damp yellow fog swirling over the city, he perspired freely, and continually wiped his brow with a cheap bandana. He seemed at once ill at ease, yet perfectly confident, if you know what I mean. I realize that it sounds like silly rot; but that is the only way I can describe him. Utterly certain that he could do that for which he had come, but very much wishing that he were anywhere else. I heard Watts-Bedloe mutter 'my word!' And I believe he would have spat disgustedly — were such an act thinkable of a physician in a London hospital!

"The Luciferian priest turned to Sir William. When he spoke, it seemed entirely in keeping with his appearance that he should take liberties with his aspirates. 'I'm 'ere, m'lord. And h'at your service.'

"Watts-Bedloe spoke sharply, 'Look here, my man!' he said. 'Do you pretend to say that you can make this crippled child whole?'

"The strange man turned his moist, pasty face, livid in the fog murk, toward the specialist. 'E that I serves can, and will. I'm a middleman, in a manner of speaking. A transmitter. H'its easy enough for 'im, but I don't advise it, and I warns you I'm not to be 'eld responsible for 'ow 'E does it.'

"Watts-Bedloe turned to Sir William. 'Let's have an end to the sickening farce,' he said curtly. 'I need fresh air!'

"Sir William nodded to the little man, who mopped his brow with his bandana, and pointed to the cot. 'Draw back the coverlet!' he commanded.

"The nurse obeyed, after a questioning glance at Watts-Bedloe. 'Tyke off 'is night gown,' continued the visitor.

"Watts-Bedloe's lips parted in a snarl at this, but Sir William arrested him with a gesture, stepped to his son's side, and with infinite gentleness took off the tiny gown, leaving the sleeping child naked in his bed.

"Again, as always, I felt a surge of pity sweep through me. The noble head, the pigeon breast, rising and falling softly now, the crooked spine, the little gnarled, twisted limbs! But my attention was quickly drawn back to the strange man.

"Barely glancing at the child, he fumbled at his greasy waistcoat, Watts-Bedloe watching him meanwhile like a lynx, as he took out a crumb of chalk and, squatting down, drew a rude circle on the floor about him; a circle of possibly four feet in diameter. And within this circle he began laboriously to write certain worked and figures."

"Hold on there!" spoke Bliven. "Certain words and figures? Just what symbols, please?"

"There was a swastika emblem," Royce promptly replied, "and others familiar to some of the older secret orders, and sometimes found on Aztec ruins and Babylonian brick tablets; the open eye, for instance, and a rude fist with thumb extended. Also he scrawled the sequence 1-

2-3-4-5-6-7-9, the '8' omitted, you notice, which he multiplied by 18, and again by 27, and by 36; you can amuse yourselves working it out. The result is curious. Lastly, he wrote the sentence, '*Sigma te, sigma, temere me tangis et angis.*' A palindrome, you observe; that is, it reads equally well — or ill, backward or forward."

"Hocus pocus! Old stuff!" snorted Bliven.

Royce gazed mildly at him.

"Old stuff, as you say, professor. Older than recorded history. Having done this, a matter of five minutes, perhaps, with Watts-Bedloe becoming more and more restless, and evidently holding himself in with difficulty, the fellow rose stiffly from his squatting position, carefully replaced the fragment of chalk in his pocket, mopped his brow for the twentieth time, and gestured toward the cot with a moist palm. 'Now, cover 'im h'up!' he ordered. 'All h'up; 'ead and all.'

"The nurse gently drew the sheet over the little form. We could see it rise and fall with the regular respiration of slumber. Suddenly, eyes wide open and staring at the floor, the fellow began to pray, in Latin. And whatever his English, his Latin was beautiful to listen to, and virgin pure! It was too voluble for me to follow verbatim — I made as good a transcript as I could a bit later, and will be glad to show it to you, Bliven — but, anyhow, it was a prayer to Lucifer, at once an adoration and a petition, that he would vouchsafe before these Christian unbelievers a proof of his dominion over fire, earth, air and water. He ceased abruptly as he had begun, and nodded toward the cot. 'H'it is done!' he sighed, and once again mopped his forehead.

"'You infernal charlatan!' snarled Watts-Bedloe, unable longer to contain himself. 'You've got the effrontery to stand there and tell us anything has been wrought upon that child by your slobbering drivel?'

"The man looked at him with lusterless eyes. 'Look for yerself, guv'ner.' he answered.

"It was Sir William who snatched back the sheet from his son; and till my dying day I shall remember the unearthly beauty of what our astounded eyes beheld. Lying there, smile upon his lips, like a perfect form fresh from the hand of his Creator, his little limbs straight and delicately rounded, a picture of almost awesome loveliness, lay the child we had but five minutes before seen as a wrecked and broken travesty of humanity."

Again Bliven interrupted explosively:

"Oh, I say now, Royce! I'll admit you tell a ripping story, as such; you had even me hanging breathless on your climax. But this is too much! As man to man, you can't sit there and tell us this child was cured!"

"I didn't say that; for he was dead."

Bliven was speechless, for once; but Holmes spoke up in remonstrance:

"It seems strange to me that such a queer story should not have been repeated, and discussed!"

"It isn't strange, if you happen to know anything about London hospitals," Royce explained patiently. "Who would repeat it? Would Watts-Bedloe permit it to be known that by his permission some charlatan was admitted, and that during his devilish incantations his patient died? Would the stricken father mention the subject, even to us? Or the head nurse and orderly, cogs in an inexorable machine?

"All this took place nearly forty years ago; and it is the first time I have spoken of it. Watts-Bedloe died years back; and Sir William's line is extinct. I can't verify a detail; but it all happened exactly as I have stated. As for the Luciferians, none of us, I think, saw him depart. He simply stole out in to the slimy yellow fog, back to whatever private hell it was he came from, somewhere in London, the city nobody knows, and where anything may happen!"

The Affair at Baker's Bluff

It is improbable that you have ever so much as heard of Baker's Bluff, a drowsy little town in mid Georgia. Its single wide street is lined with magnolias behind which may be seen ancient houses, much too large for the families who lounge upon the deck-like verandas languidly munching clingstone peaches, or "rattlers," or luscious red persimmons, according to the season, or gazing placidly upon the village common fringed with dozing mules and aged negroes. The red brick courthouse keeps guard over all.

Yet, in distant Leeds, you may hear English spinners insisting upon Baker's Bluff cotton and none other — because its fiber is a full eighth of an inch longer than that of any other upland cotton grown in Georgia.

Prosperous ten-mule farms surround the somnolent old town, and on market days, or when court is sitting, you may overhear melancholy gentlemen murmur to one another from beneath black slouch hats or sweeping panamas: "I reckoned on a good top-crop this year, suh, and Ah'll barely clear ten thousand dollars!"

Such is Baker's Bluff, and such it has ever been save for an epochal day when a wing of Sherman's army swept through long ago on its way to the sea, and suffered here a totally unimportant check which is not even mentioned in Northern histories, but which, in the belief of every true Baker's Bluffer deserves an appendix to Creasy's "Ten Decisive Battles of the World."

I have a personal reason for feeling, as far back as I can remember, an interest in the town; for it was here that my uncle, a young orderly, disappeared mysteriously during the brief affair to which the natives always refer as "*the* battle." My grandfather was a man of some wealth and influence, and made every effort to learn the fate of his son; but to no avail.

In the morning he was a dashing blade, with the longish hair and the premature beard affected in the sixties; at the next roll call, his saddle was empty. Nothing more could be learned, although several hundred obscure privates were identified, and repose under neat head-stones in the village cemetery, and are impartially decorated every year by the children, who look with indulgent pity upon the misguided vic-tims of their brilliant victory.

So, business taking me to Atlanta, I carried out a long cherished purpose, and chugged up the single track, one-train-a-day road which passes through Baker's Bluff, and struggles to keep the rust from its rails and the weeds from between them.

As there are no springs or views to attract boarders, and I could not have told a boll- weevil from a possum, I made no secret of my errand; and nothing could have exceeded the gentle courtesy of the natives, or their efforts to make me feel at home. The true Southerner talks freely of himself and his family connections, and does not understand New England reticence. Although I was a guest of the Jefferson Hotel, I cannot speak with authority of its cuisine, since I scarcely recall a meal within its genteelly shabby walls, barring breakfasts. At one or another of the town houses I dined in rotation, and by the end of the week could have acted as official guide to the battlefield.

Nobody had ever heard of my uncle's disappearance. Nobody had even heard his name; although the dear souls pretended that they had, and spoke vaguely of him as "a dashing young officer, suh!" And, not to sail under false colors, let me say right here that my visit to Baker's Bluff added nothing to the family tradition; nothing, that is, which would have been accepted by a probate court.

I can scarcely say why I lingered on. It was hot and dry, and the woods were filled with the detestable though practically invisible 'red bugs," necessitating copious paintings with iodine until I resembled a gross speckled trout. No one came to the hotel save an occasional cotton broker, or a grocery or hardware salesman. Yet I stayed on, falling under the peculiar spell of the place, tinged for me with an almost impersonal melancholy due to the unknown fate which had overtaken my uncle, whom I had never seen.

Baker's Bluff has one and only one show place, in the form of a small wooden cyclorama, dominating the town like a huge hogshead set on end. The paint has mostly peeled from its outside, since an ocean of it was required to cover its convexity, and there existed no fund for maintenance. An aged Confederate veteran was ready at all times to conduct visitors about' its circular platform and lecture upon the battle, for the sum of twenty-five cents, children fifteen cents, babes in arms free, and bona-fide citizens a dime each. This was the only source of revenue for its up-keep, and from it was deducted the guide's fees; so that it was gradually falling into a state of dry rot. If one stamped upon the platform, a cloud of dust rose like the smoke of battle.

The artist — I call him that unreservedly — who had painted the *Battle of Baker's Bluff* was an obscure French Creole from New Orleans, concerning whom I could learn nothing at all; but I maintain that in this single effort of his life he had evinced nothing short of stark genius.

The cyclorama belongs to a vanished period. It has its place in the evolution leading up to the moving picture, and belongs somewhere between the panorama and the magic lantern. It is scorned by the connoisseur because it does not hesitate to utilize every trick of perspective, and to paint a rearing cavalry horse beside a stuffed one, to mingle cunningly broken wheels, straw, rifles, dirt and rocks, tin canteens, all the litter of a battle field, with the painted canvas, in a way frankly intended to challenge the eye as to where paint ends and *props* begin.

I never lost the first breathless thrill felt when I had climbed the rickety stairs and stood with the old soldier upon the pulpit-like platform, with its sounding board, and, looking upon a scroll of canvas not over ten yards distant, rested my eyes by letting them sweep a mighty rolling countryside, to a far distant horizon. In this vast open space, the fiat echoes of our voices came as a freak of nature.

Of the lecture, I recall nothing save disjointed sentences: "Yonder, whar yo' see the white house under the gum tree, stands Gen'l Breckenridge, surveyin' the field;" or, "Gunnel Lowry is leadin' his men into action thar by the stone fence next the peach orchard —" and so forth. I heard him merely as a monotone from the past; a suitable chant, or chorus, not so much explanatory as tonal. He never failed to itemize the hundreds of gallons of paint used, and the scores of brushes worn out by the industrious artist.

The battle took place on a day made cool by numerous heavy showers; and I have come in from the sweltering June heat, to this unventilated and much hotter place, and drawn a deep breath of relief beneath its cool gray canvas skies, and seemed to feel the eternal breeze stirring miles of waving corn, and whipping the banners of forgotten legions.

Hail, Philippe Larue, who lived obscurely and died un-acclaimed, but created a masterpiece of noble conception and admirable technique!

The frowzy old cyclorama became a sort of obsession with me, and not a single day passed that I did not visit it. It seemed to sweep me into the far past, where I stood in the midst of thousands of ghosts, whose faded uniforms showed no vivid contrast of blue and gray, but were of a rusty and sun bleached uniformity which merged with the grain and the brushwood, so that my opera glasses were constantly in use to pick out the various regiments, and to identify individual faces, scores of which became as familiar to me as those of the present day denizens of the town.

Vigorous young figures, singularly matured by the straggling beards, sweeping moustaches, and proud imperials of the time, serving quaintly inefficient guns, "giving 'em a bit of grape," brandishing enormous sabers, thrusting with wicked looking bayonets. There were sharpshooters perched in tall trees with squirrel guns and telescope sights, a highly unhygienic hospital station in an old barn, and a mighty babel of petrified sound, evidenced by the open mouths of a company uttering the "Rebel yell," by the cottony puffs hanging above a concealed battery, and the neighing of spirited horses — both painted and stuffed. Philippe Larue must have been a fair carpenter and unusual taxidermist, as well as artist, since the conception was wholly his own.

Of all viewpoints, I was most fascinated by a little drama enacted before one of the old plantation houses, the headquarters of the Union general in command of the particular brigade engaged. The pictured town was very like the Baker's Bluff of today, since the surprise attack of the Confederates forced retirement before any of its houses had been destroyed. It suffered less than any other town embraced in Sherman's March.

Right before me the crisis of the "battle" took place — or rather, *didn't* take place; for an entire regiment of Yanks were resting on their arms in the field back of headquarters, while, two miles away, from a grove of red oaks, debouched the Rebel force which turned the tip of the wing of the invaders, and put them to temporary rout.

Fully aware of this, evidently, the artist had painted this section with unusual care even for him. Two or three staff officers lounged about the piazza. A pop-eyed little darkey boy peeped round the corner at them, and in the yard two soldiers were pursuing a razorback hog with felonious intent.

In the immediate foreground, sitting his horse with youthful ease, big cavalry boots thrust into loose box stirrups, an orderly was gazing earnestly up at a window in the second story of the house. Following his eyes, I beheld a beautiful girl looking down with a smile of half invitation, half defiance upon the young foeman in her front yard.

This suggestive little aside, a comedy relief to the grim war story, exercised a peculiar fascination upon me. I always sat down upon the dusty bench at this point and indulged my fancy in weaving a coherent plot on the frail basis of a pair of youthful, and probably casual glances, snatched from the serious business of the day. With no justification at all, I chose to pretend that this idle young orderly was my uncle. True, he did not in any way resemble the daguerreotype treasured by my own family, but this was no objection, since Philippe Larue had never seen him. But that there had been, at least, a romance, I presently learned from Mr. Thomas Jefferson Maxey, who occupied the very house from whose upper window the lovely girl looked forth with half startled eyes.

"The young lady in question, suh," he assured me when I spoke to him about it, "was an only daughter of one of our most respected old families. She was a Paulding, suh, and on her mother's side, an Allyn. The estate came into my possession through purchase from Judge Andy Paulding, the last of his race, who died in this town a venerable man. And the story goes that this young orderly, whose name I have forgotten if I ever knew it, was severely wounded here, and was nursed back to strength by this same young lady you may see in the window. The war was ovah befo' he recovered, and they were married. Such was the story told to Larue, at the time he gathered the facts for the cyclorama, suh."

No one was able to add anything to this tradition, and some repudiated it altogether. The young couple, if indeed they married, had never dwelt in the old house, which had descended to another branch of the family.

It amused me to sit here on sweltering afternoons, under the meretricious coolness of the painted clouds, with the ancient guide dozing in the entrance below, and fancy that my uncle had been struck down here, and after a long illness, possibly having lost his memory from the effects of the minié ball which it was said struck his head — and the minié balls I had seen in museums appeared about the size of walnuts — had wedded the lovely Southern girl, and begun life under a new name.

I found myself scrutinizing the tow-headed youngsters who rode into town on market days atop of wagonloads of produce, trying to identify the famous Adams nose. There were varieties enough; freckled, pug, more or less in need of the friendly services of a handkerchief, sometimes; but nothing that my romantic hopes could identify with any of the features of my uncle, or our characteristic family type in general.

I sat, one sultry day, in my regular place where I idled away a half hour daily, and although I felt cool, as a psychological reaction, nevertheless I must have had, not of course a sunstroke, but a touch of vertigo; for suddenly, I left my hard bench, and vaulted lightly into the painted saddle of my friend the young orderly. My ears were nearly deafened by the instant transition from utter silence to the clamor of battle. But I knew perfectly well who I was, and why there. I was young Lieutenant Amos Adams, with an urgent message from my harassed colonel, sorely pressed by a surprise attack from the oak grove, to head-quarters, asking supports from the regiment held in reserve about the old Paulding house.

The general, it seemed, had cantered off a moment before, with several of his staff; and would be back at headquarters in a jiffy. Mean-while, my eyes lifted, and I looked into those of a young woman stand-ing by. They seemed a little contemptuous, somewhat hostile; and yet, there was a subtle invitation there, as well! And did not the sleek head with its golden, cane-syrup colored locks parted severely and brushed back over the smooth low brow to be held in place by an absurdly big tortoise shell comb — did not this altogether delectable little head ges-ture, almost imperceptibly, back and over one shoulder? And needed ever a gay young warrior more than this to set his spurred boots clat-tering up wooden stairs, or across drawbridges, or scaling rope ladders?

1 glanced around with a swiftly comprehensive, military omni-science. Far to my rear, the colonel seemed to be holding his own. The general had not yet returned. I could be at his side when he did so, be-fore he had brought his horse to a stand before the door. The officers on the piazza were watching the pursuit of the razorback hog.

I tossed my reins to a little darkey, dismounted, and turned unob-served into the door at the end of the roomy old house. The fine old mahogany furniture was in some disorder. A great round table had been dragged to the center of the room, and was covered with maps. A pair of riding gloves and a pistol held down the curling edges of one of these. Beyond the fireplace, a stairway led to the floor above. The girl I found in that silent room uttered no word of greeting. She put one hand to her heart, as I entered, sweeping the floor with my visored cap. For a mo-ment we stared at one another, like a couple of school children. Then I moved towards her.

She was pale, even serious; but her lips carried an enigmatic smile. As I advanced, she undulated back towards the fireplace corresponding to the one in the room below. Her great, balloon-like crinoline skirt seemed to float across the floor, her tiny bronze colored slippers appearing and disappearing noiselessly, the big cameo upon her bosom rising and falling with her breathing. Suddenly, she paused, placing a finger to her lips, a startled look flitting across her pale face. She was listening intently.

"Hark!" she whispered, head inclined towards the door by which I had entered. "If you are seen here, I declare I am undone!"

I heard nothing, but stopped and listened; and so realistic was her action, that when she turned swiftly, and with nimble fingers plucked at the paneling beside the fireplace, and pulled open an unsuspected door, I permitted her to take my sleeve and urge me towards it. At the very entrance, I became suspicious, and stopped, half turning; but a crushing blow on my head scattered my wits, and I was violently thrust into utter darkness!

As I passed out on the tide of oblivion, with the slam of the door in my ears, I could have sworn that I heard a strangled sob, and the words — "oh — I *had* to do it, boy!"

What I did hear, beyond peradventure, was the anxious drawl of the old guide in my ear. He was shaking my shoulder, and a little tobacco juice was trickling down his grizzled chin.

"I reackon it's powerful hot in yere today, sonny," he said. "Heerd ye a talkin' to yo'self, and come up. Yo' want to get out, an' git ye a mouthful o' fresh air!"

I roused from the stupor into which I had fallen, and allowed him to lead me down to the outer air, which immediately restored me, as the sun was low, and a little breeze was stirring up the quiet street.

I had stayed on at Baker's Bluff a most unconscionable time. The children had ceased to regard me as an imported curio, and all the town darkies knew me by name. In short, I had ceased to be regarded as a newcomer, and, in fact, was now considered to be a citizen in good standing. At the old hotel, it had ceased to rouse comment when I insisted on sugar and milk for my grits, instead of hot pork fat. I had eaten my fill of beaten biscuits and corn pone and native bacon and waffles and sorghum. I made ready to depart.

Before leaving, however, I begged my friend Mr. Thomas Jefferson Maxey, to permit me to visit the room in whose window Larue had painted the little lady with the inviting eyes. He agreed cordially, and preceded me upstairs, puffing a little, for he was well stricken in flesh.

The room was reserved, he explained, as a guest chamber. He added, with characteristic native hospitality, that he would consider it an honor if I would occupy it for as long as I chose to remain.

With shutters drawn, it looked cool and restful with the dull gleam of old mahogany, and against its paneled walls I noted a few family portraits; but none of the girl I could not put out of my mind.

After a glance from the self-same window from which she had lured my — me — well, in which Larue had painted her, I turned inquiringly to my host.

"There was a sort of secret closet, was there not? Over to the left of the fireplace?"

His light blue eyes widened in genuine surprise. For a moment he hesitated before replying to my inquiry.

"Why, no suh; no such tradition exists, suh!"

I crossed over, and scrutinized the fine old panels close to the mantelpiece. Almost, I could see the very spot touched by the fluttering fingers of the little girl of long ago. My own engaged themselves busily about the beveled edges.

Suddenly, a segment of the wall seemed to lean in upon me. I stepped hastily back, and a heavy door, solid as that of a big refrigerator, opened out. I heard a wheeze of amazement behind me; and my host scuffed across the floor to my side. Together, we gazed into a dark, windowless room, or perhaps it would be more fitting to call it a cupboard, about six feet in depth.

It was empty, save for the dust of years which lay upon the floor; or so we thought at first. Presently, as my eyes grew accustomed to the obscurity within, I entered, and from the far corner brought forth an old tin canteen, its sides velvety with rust.

The Old Man of the Sea

Those hornets of France, the *Chasseurs Alpins*, had brought in a rare prize on their last trench raid, in the person of a Brandenburg colonel who was inspecting his first line of defense. Such trout were seldom drawn among the minnows; and a peculiar relish was added by the fact that Von Eckmeyer, the prisoner, had ordered and supervised the terrible reprisals visited upon the little Belgian hamlets, three of which had since been recaptured by the French.

The boches, as usual, claimed that there had been provocation by *francs tireurs*. It is possible that some half-crazed peasant may have lost what few remaining wits he had, and fired an impotent shot from some rusty fowling piece; the fact is relatively unimportant.

With Teutonic thoroughness the capable Oberst von Eckmeyer set about his task of so branding divers lovely little villages that future visitors, though perfectly able to conceive what manner of men had passed that way, should in no wise be able to picture what manner of folk had dwelt there.

Nay, more; that when its wretched survivors should creep back to fumble amid the broken shards and ashes, they themselves should be unable to mete out the boundaries of their stone houses, which had clustered about the ancient church unchanged since the days of Charles the Bold.

The scene, as the prisoner was conducted to headquarters, revealed a singular departure from accepted dramatic tradition. Any capable stage manager, producing this entrance, would have surrounded the colonel by a scowling mob, thrust back by the soldiery; nor would have failed to drill them in that low, menacing growl which was strangely lacking from the silent old men and women, the ill-nourished children, who gazed with a certain dreadful curiosity upon the being who had wreaked such woe in their simple lives.

So, with no reproach, no insult heaped upon him, he came at length to the rough wooden shelter which served as the officers' quarters and where there were at present a certain number gathered to determine what disposition should be made of the bloody persecutor chance and the *Chasseurs Alpins* had brought to them.

They saluted punctiliously as he was brought in, and were saluted in return.

The boche colonel was a fine type of the male animal, bred to war as dogs to the chase. His florid face bore the scars of his old university days as member of a fighting corps. The back of his bullet-like head was as flat as one's hand, and crowned by a stiff brush of blond hair. His blue eyes were fearless and intelligent; upon his broad chest reposed several orders.

This was he who had diligently and methodically martyred six villages and their inhabitants. And because life is a texture of inconsistencies which cease to be incongruous when once they are regarded attentively, there were presently found among his papers the fond likenesses of his gentle-hearted wife and his pretty children, with loving and laudatory letters from the distant town where he was known as a kind neighbor and a devout Christian.

When he had been carefully searched, and had answered their queries with contemptuous silence, the senior French officer quietly introduced the subject of the recent barbarities.

"In view, *Herr Oberst*, of the excellent discipline maintained by your troops, it can scarcely be doubted that the recent reprisals upon the people whose homes formerly stood hereabout, were inflicted by command, and could not have been spontaneous acts?"

Von Eckmeyer gazed vacantly upon his French interrogator from the monocle he wore upon a black ribbon.

"It is a question we cannot justly expect the *Herr Oberst* to answer, monsieurs," protested a grizzled major of the line. "Observe that he feels himself in a hostile environment. A natural instinct of shame, and fear as well, silences his prudent tongue!"

The Brandenburger flushed. The insinuation unsealed lips that no tortures could have compelled to reveal a military secret He squared his broad shoulders.

"What is done, is done," he remarked succinctly. "It is merciful to teach non-combatants the dangers of sniping. Also, it hastens the day of universal peace. War is terrible. The sooner its horrors are realized, the sooner will madmen cease to fight against God and destiny."

The major elevated his thin shoulders, thrusting forth his hands in a gesture of assent.

"This is the voice of wisdom and compassion," he agreed. "He would inflict a little misery, in order to avoid greater miseries. When we occupied what is left on this village, we found the body of a nun crucified upon the door of her convent. Behold — here is the photograph — the *oberst* will recognize it!"

He held up a picture, recorded by the mellow sunshine of Flanders. The German gazed upon it unflinchingly.

"He has conferred an immortal crown upon our sister," the major continued. "In the days of Nero, men and women craved the boon of martyrdom, and even begged that they might be crucified head downward, lest their blessed sacrifice bear too close a resemblance to the death of *notre seigneur*. Yet, in his far-seeing mercy, he would not see this earthly distress prolonged unduly.

"*Par exemple*, he would grieve to return to his home and find his wife, whose photograph we have also looked upon, crucified against the door of his ruined mansion; as also, the right hands of his little sons cut off, lest they grow up to bear arms against the invader of the fatherland. It is even so! The look in his eyes confesses it.

"His hand smites that strife may pass from our midst. These broken plowshares, these girdled trees, are mute witnesses to his beneficent desire that our young men shall busy themselves in vineyard and smithy, rather than in munitions plant and armory. The deaths of our aged and infirm serve but to remove from our shoulders the burden of their support. Am I not just *Herr Oberst*?"

The prisoner replied neither by word nor change of expression. He stood immobile as one of those wooden figures of Hindenburg into which admirers drive iron nails.

For a moment or so the French officers whispered together about their plain wooden table. Then, nodding to an orderly:

"Bring in M. le Maire Houcken," the chief commanded.

Despite his iron self-control, the German started violently at these words. For he, with his own eyes, had beheld the old man Houcken hanged, and afterward had seen one of his shriveled arms protruding from the shallow grave into which they had tumbled him.

Old Houcken had been a fisherman all his life. In his lusty youth none had pulled a stronger oar, or steered a straighter course. He came to own his own sloop, then two, and finally four. For his village, he was reckoned wealthy.

When war swept over his country he assumed the duties of mayor for his own and a number of little surrounding hamlets. He spent himself freely, did all that was humanly possible to relieve suffering and allay fear, and in due time fell beneath the wheels of the German juggernaut, and was executed as a prominent citizen-hostage.

He had met his fate, not in his native village, which was farther to the north on the coast, but in the town which two days later was retaken by the French, and where the military council was now examining his executioner.

Von Eckmeyer instantly regained his *sang-froid*, and waited phlegmatically for whatever might result from the amazing order of his examiner.

There presently sounded on the wooden planking laid over the mud before the building the heavy tramp of men; and, a slight breeze setting in through the open door from the west, there was wafted into the room a sickening odor too familiar to all gathered therein. With almost superhuman resolution, the German colonel held his eyes to the front as the newcomers entered.

Two soldiers bore between them, brawny hands beneath its shoulders, the body of an old, gray-bearded man. It was Houcken, the mayor, taken from the hastily scooped grave where he had lain for three days. His feet clear of the floor, the mud not even brushed from his clothes or his matted hair, he was carried to a position squarely facing the prisoner, and held up a bare yard from him.

Simultaneously, the French officers rose and saluted; and some slight movement of the supporting soldiers disturbing his relaxed joints and sinews, the ghastly figure bowed its head as if in courteous acknowledgment.

Because he had been hanged, his swollen, purple tongue protruded; the mildew of the grave had not yet washed out the salt and iodine encrusted upon his face by fifty years of sea fog and Channel spray. His eyelids were wide open. One empty socket testified to the temerity of some epicurean raven, or to a m6re sinister mishap; beneath the dull glaze of death upon his single eye, those who observed fancied they could still trace the indomitable courage of the spirit which had fled.

Despite himself, the prisoner recoiled slightly; and in the silence of the little room could be heard the faint tinkle of the orders upon his breast; the Iron Cross girding upon the order pour la mérite, the latter upon the Prussian Eagle.

"The *Herr Oberst*," spoke the presiding officer," is free to return to his lines. Widely as his views of military expediency differ from ours, it is not for us to judge an officer for obeying orders. *C'est la guerre.* Nor is it our purpose to subject him to any humiliation. His private papers and personal property, saving only his side arms, will be restored, and he will presently be escorted to No-Man's Land, which he will cross, under flag of truce, to his command."

The Brandenburger sought to evade the appalling regard of the dead man, who seemed to deride him with out-thrust tongue, leering into his face with an air of senile cunning. As often as he forced his gaze to rest upon the features of the speaker, seeking to read there the hidden menace he instinctively felt lay beneath his fair words, so often did it return to the grinning horror that confronted him.

"One little service," the officer continued, "we ask in return for liberty. The desire to lay one's bones in native soil is one of the most universal and enduring of human instincts. This old man loved his sea. The town where he was born, and lived, and where his ancestors — those who escaped drowning — lie buried, is now within your lines. Let me say rather, that the site of this town is there. I am imposing on you, Oberst von Eckmeyer, the duty of bearing this man with you, to be interred in his own sod. There is no further requirement. You will now be escorted to the front."

He nodded; and instantly two squat Breton infantrymen stepped forward, and with deft fingers bound the prisoner's arms immovably to his sides, fastening the loose ends with cunning knots. He struggled against the indignity; but even his great strength was as nothing in the blunt, hairy hands of the Bretons.

Next, the limp form of the old man was placed breast to breast with him, and firmly lashed to his body, its arms and legs free, the feet clearing the ground.

On Von Eckmeyer's face a profuse sweat broke out, and ran in little trickles down his temples, and the deep channels from nose to lips. The ruddy flush of health died slowly out of his face as it confronted that of his horrible incubus, but a few inches from his own.

"In medieval days," the even tones of the French officer again broke the silence, "in cases of homicide accompanied by unusual circumstances of cruelty, the body of the victim was sometimes bound to his slayer, who was then turned loose to wander where he would until he contracted from his loathsome burden the one incurable disease — *death*. No such purpose animates us. In half an hour at most, you will be with your own men."

Obedient to the directions of a young lieutenant, Von Eckmeyer turned and followed him steadily out of the room. Behind him the two Bretons came, with fixed bayonets.

Outside the sun shone genially. There was little local cannonading; the thrilling song of a lark was clearly audible as it winged its way skyward. In two long lines, stretching far to the eastward, were drawn up the soldiery, eyes to the front, arms at the present.

Little groups of peasantry watched with haggard eyes the strange scene, children clinging to their mothers' homespun kirtles. Between the lines walked the Branded burger with proud and unfaltering tread, his face pale and bedewed with sweat, but his demeanor uncowed.

And as he marched on between the silent ranks, a strange thing was noted. The loose members of the old man, three days buried, flapped rhythmically; while his head twisted from side to side with the uncanny flexibility of a parrot's.

Now he seemed to whisper in Von Eckmeyer's ear some rare and nameless graveyard jest; one of the secrets Lazarus so carefully guarded upon his resurrection. Then, leaning back, he would seem to leer waggishly at his bearer, as if seeking to discover in his face some signs of approbation.

And again, he would rest his corrupt head upon the broad breast, adorned with its honorable orders, in a grisly and maudlin confidence. Never for an instant was he at rest; never, when not in actual contact with Von Eckmeyer's face, more than a few inches from it.

So, at a pace as smart as his bonds and his burden permitted, he came at length to the first trench, and from it entered the intricate system of communication trenches.

Sentries saluted as they filed past; earth-colored cloths were raised, and glittering eyes scrutinized them from the dark interiors of bomb-proofs. In due time they attained the first trench, where already a great white flag had attracted the curiosity of the Germans squatting in their shelters a bare hundred yards away.

Over the top stepped Von Eckmeyer, alone now with the old man he bore, and recognized instantly by the sharp eyes of his own men.

Knowing themselves safe until the *oberst* should have crossed to his own lines, heads began to appear above the French trench; and presently from the German trench as well. Powerful stereo-binoculars were trained on the singular pair, that no detail should be lost, no change of expression missed.

Halfway across No Man's Land, picking his way carefully amid the shell craters, it was observed that Von Eckmeyer's knees were quivering. It is the knees which fight-fans watch at a pugilistic combat; for these play the traitor while yet eyes are true, and body and face unmarked. Von Eckmeyer began to stumble a very little.

And suddenly, so that those who watched caught their breaths sobbingly, he stopped, and in a powerful and sonorous voice, began to sing. And the song was an old drinking chorus familiar to all German students. One could fairly hear the thumping of steins upon oak, and smell the fumes of beer and the acrid smoke of strong porcelain pipes.

The song finished, the Brandenburger began to dance, clumsily, like a great bear. Doubtless it was long since he had waived his dignity thus, and besides, he was hampered by what was bound tightly to his body. But no such handicap affected the old man.

With a horrible and unnatural agility, the corpse, its feet never quite touching the ground, began to dance in time to Von Eckmeyer's steps. Its arms flapped loosely; its thin legs, apparently joint-less, threw themselves about with epileptic abandon, its lolling head beat time to the danse macabre.

It gave every indication of an uncanny and obscene delight in the pastime, out there in No Man's Land, where the unburied French and German raiders lay side by side in the democracy of death.

To more than one observer came the unbidden thought that, had old Houcken been able in life to do what his poor cadaver was doing now, he could have earned in a single month a larger sum than he had wrested from the sea in half a century of bitter toil!

Abruptly, the officer stopped, and for an instant stood motionless, his face — as it chanced — turned toward the foe. They noted that his eyes were closed; and that a little froth bubbled from between his parted lips.

Very slowly, reluctantly it seemed, he fell forward; and as this was toward and upon the body of the old man, the singular illusion that the latter was gradually pulling him down, overcoming his great thews by the patient inertia of death, was impressed upon the eyes of the beholders.

It was at this moment of dramatic horror that an unprecedented climax was added by the swarming of the bodies from their shelter, distant but a scant sixty yards.

The Teutons are not given to voluntary exposure. They leave their holes only when compelled to do so: bravely enough, but more like a herd of cattle than like inspired warriors.

Now, however, either because they were beside themselves at sight of the ghastly predicament of their colonel, or because some quick-thinking petty officer thought the occasion ripe for a surprise attack, they rushed pell-mell toward the enemy trench.

Military tactics indicated a machine gun fire which would have exterminated them before they could have reached the barbed wire; but the Plan of the French carried them over the top to meet the enemy in No Man's Land. They met, in fact, before the German *oberst* and his gruesome burden had time to topple to the ground; so that, sustained by the mass of struggling men, they were borne hither and yon, and yet steadily toward the boche trench.

To those who caught fleeting glimpses of them it seemed now that the officer was endeavoring to carry out his mission by bearing the old man home, and again that the dead man was by some occult force dragging the Brandenburger through the thick of the fight toward his own lines. No one could tell how it was that they passed the barrier; but when the surprise attack had failed, and the French remained in possession of the trench, the two were found on the inner side.

And there, come at length to his own village, the old man of the sea was interred. And there also they buried the *oberst*; and as a final touch of irony in a grim business, it was noted that whereas the inert flesh of the Mayor Houcken was riddled with wounds, the body of the Brandenburger, fair in death, bore no mark whatever save where the cord had bound him tightly!

The Goat of Dolores Valdez

To the chief inquisitor, Don Rafael, came the fat little assistant, with trouble in his twinkling eyes.

"Illustrious," he said, "the milk girl will not reveal anything!"

Don Rafael sighed, and laid aside the thick roll of parchment on which he was laboriously transcribing his "Life of St. Francis of Assisi," the dearest project of his latter years.

He was a kindly, handsome old man, with a pink skin and snow-white hair.

To his assistant's remarks he replied simply: "She must!"

He opened a drawer in his ebony and tortoise-shell cabinet, and removed from it a formidable-looking document, adangle with awkward red seals the size of Spanish dollars. Spreading it before him he refreshed his memory of Dolores Valdez.

She was, it appeared from the document, a simple peasant girl, of less than twenty years; poor, her only possession being a goat, which she daily drove to the houses of her customers, and milked into the pitchers and jugs they brought to her.

She was an orphan, and was not known to have any living relative.

In some curious fashion she had become entangled with a body of dangerous conspirators, who used her as a messenger, her poverty and obscurity causing her to be ignored by the secret police. That she received from her fees as messenger more than from the sale of her goat's milk, was known; also, that she had bound herself by terrible oaths not to betray the names of her employers.

Their plans were unknown to her; but she was in possession of the names and descriptions of many criminals, several of whom had taken part in a recent unsuccessful attempt upon the life of the queen mother.

For the past two weeks Dolores Valdez had resisted every effort to force her to reveal the names of the conspirators.

It was with a full realization of the importance of the affair that the chief inquisitor had replied to his worried assistant's statement with the words: "She must!"

He finished reading the document, replaced it carefully in the table-drawer, glanced with a parting sigh at his "Life of St. Francis," and asked: "Is she pretty?"

The assistant coughed. "She — was," he replied.

"Well, what has been done with her? What has she said?"

"Everything and nothing," the assistant answered both queries. "First, an effort was made to discover some relative, and failing that, some friend that they might be tortured before her eyes, so that she would reveal the desired information rather than see her own flesh and blood suffer. The utmost efforts of the secret police did not avail to find one relative, and stranger yet, one intimate."

Don Rafael shook his head incredulously.

"You say she is — was — pretty; the document mentions her as having, for a peasant, unusual intelligence; and yet there was no young man, no young girl, beloved of her?"

The assistant answered: "Pallacio himself took up the search, and could find no one."

"Well, what next was done?"

"She was made intoxicated with strong wine of Xeres, in the hope that under its influence she might forget herself. I regret to sky that, although she at last became quite ill, she never lost her head. Illustrious, I would give my farm in Andalusia for her capacity!"

"Well — and then?"

"Then she was kept continuously awake for a week. But though she became so exhausted that she would fall asleep with her eyes wide open and the hot iron on her flesh, her nerves never gave way. She would answer nothing."

"Was this all?"

"At last she was subjected to the question by water; first, of course, the question ordinary; but later, the question extraordinary. She defied us, and, when she was able to speak, she cursed us.

"So you see that everything possible has been done. Yet she is the only one who can give the police the information needed, and each day renders the escape of the conspirators more probable."

"Did you come here, my son, to explain these things to me, or to seek my assistance?" Don Rafael asked, with gentle irony.

The assistant was properly abashed.

"Unless you help us, we shall kill her without getting a word!" he declared.

"That would be a pity, for two reasons: no one wishes to see a little peasant girl who delivered messages she could not read, abused or killed; and certainly she must be made to speak, I fear I shall have to induce her myself. I had hoped that my servants might save me this trouble, but it would seem that they are singularly lacking in intelligence."

If lacking in intelligence, however, the chief inquisitor's servants were not lacking in industry, or in equipment. At this very moment, Pedro, the tormentor, was pouring out to his wife in their snug cabin near the city gate, his troubles with the refractory dairymaid. The honest fellow sat by the fire with his youngest girl on his knee, while the wife prepared his simple but wholesome dinner.

As a good wife, she sympathized with him, consoled him, suggested expedients; interlarding her advice with curses on the thick-headed peasant girl who was causing her beloved so much grief and disappointment.

Poor peasant girl! Lying on a rough pallet in the chamber of torture beneath the municipal palace, thankful for a brief respite, she longed to be in the sunshine again, followed by her little goat, and pausing to fill the stone crock of some customer and receive therefore a tiny copper coin.

Of a hardy race, and in splendid health, she had borne stoically the pains inflicted upon her by Pedro. For these she had prepared herself before the ordeal, and steeled her soul.

Intensely superstitious, she thoroughly believed that her soul was lost forever were she to break the dreadful oaths she had been forced to take, and reveal her employers; and she was determined to die by inches if so it must be, and save her soul alive. She had tried to imagine every possible horror, every frightful and subtle wrench of nerve and muscle; if possible the reality was less terrible than her fancies, and it had not been too hard to hold her peace, though her sufferings under the question extraordinary had been frightful and prolonged, so that she had fainted.

Probably no member of Dolores's tough-fibered family had fainted prior to this for several centuries.

When it came to the waking test, however, resistance had been harder; indeed, had Pedro but known it, there was a period when she was near yielding; when she was almost prepared to barter her immortal soul for an hour's sleep.

Not once during the entire unforgettable week was she allowed a moment's sleep; there was always a patient watcher to jog her elbow, shake her, apply smelling salts beneath her nose if necessary — as it was toward the end of the third day — to pinch her flesh in one of the devilishly refined instruments of Pedro's armory.

At the end, it had been hell; she was nearly insane, and she knew that mere physical pain could never compare with prolonged insomnia. There is a point, long in coming to be sure, where nerves cease to react to stimuli of pain; but the hideous exhaustion, mental and physical, that follows sleeplessness of long duration, can neither be described nor imagined.

It was because she began to babble incoherently that Pedro gave up the test; he felt that a little longer, and she would become deranged, and unable to tell them what they must know. Lying there on her pallet, grateful for a brief respite while the assistant consulted with the mighty chief inquisitor, she wondered what fresh ingenuity would be devised to loose her tongue. That she was doomed to die, she never doubted; that no bodily pain should force her to deliver her immortal soul over to the grinning fiends who inspired the cruel Pedro, she was determined. She was glad that none of her family were left.

Were they to torture her father, years now in heaven, or her little lame brother, whom she could barely remember, or her sainted mother, she knew that she should tell them all they asked, and give her soul for the loved one; this would be simple duty. But not for her own ease and comfort would she do so!

She knew why the assistant had gone; as she lay exhausted, and with closed eyes, she had heard him tell Pedro go to his dinner, and that when he returned the chief inquisitor, who had never failed to extort a confession, would be brought to deal with the refractory creature their own cunning had failed to shake.

Little Dolores Valdez came near to smiling.

Well, she thought, here was one time the wonderful man was going to fail; doubtless he could give her nerves a severer twinge, a more unspeakable agony, than these others; else he would not be chief of them; but she was prepared for any degree of pain.

Had she not fainted away when it became unbearable? Well, she would bear it again, and in silence, up to this point; and she would faint as many times as they chose. She hoped it would kill her soon; and she hoped above all that they would not try again the waking test.

If they did, she feared for her soul; but probably they would not, as she had withstood it once, and it took many days, and time was precious to them; this she knew from their impatience.

They were not unnecessarily harsh with her, outside of the tortures; they regarded her, in fact, as a subject, as material to weld to their uses and purposes.

Pedro, it is true, felt hurt and humiliated at his non-success, but he had for Dolores herself no feeling whatever, whether of anger or admiration or sympathy.

While she was steeling her soul anew and summoning all her fortitude, Don Rafael was sadly putting away his beloved manuscript, with thoughts dwelling more on the blessed St. Francis than on the little dairymaid.

"They found nothing in her effects?" he asked absent-mindedly, as he rose to accompany his assistant.

"She owns nothing in the world beyond a few coins she has saved up, and which are now in the police archives, and the clothes on her back. Nothing, that is," he added, "but the goat. They took her while she was milking it, and it is shut up in the palace stable."

A sudden gleam illuminated Don Rafael's face, and then died out, as if a ray of sunshine had fallen across his sweet and benevolent features. He gathered his crimson robe in his hand, and said:

"Well, let us see little Dolores, and induce her to find her tongue."

Thorough and searching as had been the methods of the assistant and his faithful Pedro, indomitable and unshaken as Dolores remained, there existed in his mind not the slightest shadow of a doubt but that Don Rafael, their beloved chief inquisitor, would succeed where they had failed.

All who knew him gave him equally of their love and their confidence. For sheer intellect, he had no peer in Spain; beneath a nature gentle and unspoiled as a little child's, he had garnered a marvelous knowledge of human nature.

Singularly enough, his profound knowledge of mankind, and his official position as chief inquisitor, had neither rendered him cynical nor suspicious. Now, as he reluctantly turned from the gentle transcription which delighted his old age, he bent upon the problem before him all the powers of his remarkable mind.

So softly did he enter the chamber of torture that Dolores, who had fallen asleep, did not at once awaken; and he bent over her with the rare smile that was in itself almost a blessing.

For a long time he examined her curiously; noted where her firm, wholesome young flesh had been torn; glanced casually at the great funnel used in the torture by water, and which had been carelessly tossed to one side; gazed understanding at the deep circles beneath her closed eyes, reminiscent of her terrible and prolonged sleeplessness; studied the firm, brave young mouth, un-relaxed even in sleep, noted the strong jaw, the broad, low forehead; and finally he touched her shoulder gently.

Dolores Valdez awakened instantly, and without any start! This also he noted.

Their eyes met; and, though she had never seen the chief inquisitor, she knew him at once, and feared his wonderfully sweet smile more than the scowling brows of the brutal Pedro, who entered at this moment, brushing from his doublet the crumbs of black bread and cheese which remained from his dinner.

"My daughter," began Don Rafael, "I wish to save you from further pain, as 1 would gladly have saved you from any, I wish to send you forth into the sunshine and the streets, with your little goat. You need never work again, however, and you can deck yourself with fine clothes for the rest of your life. Tell us the things we must know, and go in peace."

Dolores Valdez shook her head, and smiled back at him, yet fearfully

"It is because of your oath?" he asked her gently, patting her brown hand. "It is because of this, and not because these men are friends of yours?"

She nodded, her head.

"Then that is all settled!" cried Don Rafael, with a confidence he was far from feeling. "Father Bonifazio shall absolved you from this oath; the Cardinal Perez, if you prefer — yes, the Holy Father himself shall send you his full absolution."

Again Dolores shook her head.

"It was such an oath, your excellency," she said, "as God Himself could not absolve me from were I to break it."

"But that is blasphemy, my daughter!"

Dolores sighed, and closed her eyes.

The chief inquisitor recognized the uselessness of further effort along this line. The clever conspirators had so framed their oaths, and so adapted them to her ignorant, obstinate little peasant's mind, that no form of absolution could convince her.

Don Rafael asked for a stool, and sat by her side. Drawing from his years and years of experience as chief inquisitor, he described to her the most terrible and excruciating tortures which it was in their power to inflict upon her.

She was shaken, despite her indomitable will, because Don Rafael was a persuasive man, as well as an imaginative and fluent conversationalist; but it was her flesh which quivered, not her spirit. That rose and defied him from her steadfast eyes.

Finally, when he felt that his purpose had been as well achieved as might be, Don Rafael called for the two recording secretaries. They came instantly, black-gowned figures, with huge inkpots and quill pens, and leaves of rustling parchment. One on each side of Dolores, they sat themselves down.

"Dip your pens in ink," Don Rafael commanded them. "Have all ready. You will need to write at top speed to take down the names and addresses Dolores Valdez will shortly give you.

Despite herself, the victim shuddered at his tone of confidence, and at the matter-of-fact expectancy of the two secretaries.

Standing beneath his array of instruments, Pedro waited inquiringly. The chief inquisitor did not so much as glance at him.

"Place the Senorita Dolores in the stocks," continued Don Rafael.

It was done in a few seconds. Her strong, well-formed feet were held firmly out. Her arms were left free.

The two secretaries nibbled reflectively at their quill pens. The assistant followed the preparations with unconcealed eagerness and curiosity. Pedro waited, silent and prepared.

"Have someone bring in a pail of strong brine," was the next command; and when it appeared, the chief inquisitor bade Pedro, with a stiff brush, apply a coating to the soles of Dolores Valdez's feet.

When it had somewhat dried, he added another, and yet another.

Dolores gazed steadfastly upon Don Rafael, who, as often as he glanced at her, smiled benevolently; once he patted her hand encouragingly.

At last he beckoned to Pedro, and whispered something in his ear; and Pedro, with astonished eyes, backed from the room.

Leisurely Don Rafael paced up and down, his mind straying back longingly to his pleasant study, and his half-finished "Life of St. Francis."

He had nearly forgotten the case in hand; he regarded it as already finished. But the whispered message, the departure of Pedro, the long delay, were agony for Dolores, and were even painful to the assistant. The two recording secretaries might have been mere manikins, for any emotion they displayed.

Presently there came a curious sound from the corridor outside the chamber of torture. The wooden shoes of Pedro, the hoarse voice of Pedro, were heard, but with them, another sound less easy to identify; a series of mincing, tapping little steps, as of two or three children walking on wooden stilts.

A moment later Pedro entered the room, leading a small, white goat.

A little cry escaped Dolores's lips. She feared anything; that they might be going to abuse the poor little creature that had served her so long and faithfully, that pity might wrench from her lips the secrets that pain had not been able to loose.

The goat saw her at once, and knew her; it bleated its pleasure and came to where she was lying, wagging its tail and licking her hand with its tongue.

Tears flowed from Dolores's eyes; she feared to betray any affection for it, and, to dissemble her real feelings, she pushed it rudely away, with a harsh word.

The chief inquisitor saw, and understood. He smiled benignantly.

Then, gently urging the goat, he led it to the foot of Dolores's pallet, and allowed it to touch her bare brown feet, firmly held in the stocks. In a few seconds, the goat discovered that these feet were covered with delicious salt; and, with every evidence of satisfaction, he began to lick them with his rough tongue.

A spasm passed over Dolores's face.

Prepared for torture, she was thrown off her guard; her toes curled convulsively. She tried to wrench her feet through the stocks; rose up and tried to beat the goat away with her hands; called to him; writhed frantically from side to side, and suddenly — a horrible sound to be heard in that chamber of torture — she burst into peals of laughter, which rapidly became hysterical.

She frothed at the lips, and her eyes seemed to be bursting from her head; the veins in her neck swelled under the pressure of blood.

Just as she seemed to be passing into a convulsion, Don Rafael drew back the goat, which struggled to get at the salt again.

The chief inquisitor made a furtive sign to the two secretaries; they dipped their quill-pens afresh.

Then, when Dolores had quieted down, and her sobbing breath was nearly normal. Don Rafael led the goat once more to her feet.

It was, perhaps, a surprise to everyone present except Don Rafael himself, that without warning, Dolores began to shriek and cry, and to babble forth names and addresses at such a rate that the recording secretaries wrote for dear life; once, as she hesitated, Don Rafael made as if to release the goat, and the confession recommenced.

At last it was ended; for "there is nothing more," Dolores sobbed; and, "I know it, my daughter!" Don Rafael replied, and instantly released her from the stocks, and lifted her tenderly to her feet.

After all, the wisest of men do not know all there is to be known of the simplest of women; and even the good chief inquisitor was surprised when, after a momentary silence, Dolores burst into frenzied screams and imprecations, cursing the day she was born, cursing the conspirators who made her take the oath, cursing Don Rafael, who made her break it.

"You have ruined me!" she wailed, when she had fairly worn herself out.

"Instead, my child, I have saved you," he replied.

"You have destroyed my soul!"

"Nay, my daughter, I have but tickled your soles!"

In vain he sought to console her; to assure her that her confession was not voluntary; that whatever form of absolution she wished should be hers.

She wept and stormed, outburst after outburst sweeping over her like waves; and far down the corridor, when she was set free with the white goat, her cries drowned the sound of its little tapping steps.

The lower jaw of Pedro was yet agape; the two secretaries were already sanding their manuscripts, ere the astonished assistant found his voice.

"Illustrious, you are marvelous!" he cried in genuine admiration. "None save you could have extorted the confession, and she would have died under our hands in silence and obstinacy of heart!"

"There is nothing marvelous about this affair," replied the chief inquisitor gently, "save that a tired old man must leave his beloved task because his servants lack a little imagination, and go through the world with their eyes closed, and force him to do their work after them.

"In fact," he concluded, as the rare smile illuminated his face, "in the case of the Senorita Dolores Valdez, it was simply a question of — getting her goat!"

The Getaway

"There goes one who is either a professional equilibrist or a pick-pocket," remarked Lapierre to me. "He's a stranger in Paris, too. Were it not that I confine myself to my special work, I'd detail a *flic* to follow him up."

We were lingering on a bench in the Jardin du Luxembourg as he indicated a medium-sized, compact gentleman whose walk and bearing had attracted my friend's attention. The stranger seemed to move aimlessly, yet without a trace of wasted motion, as if he had nothing on earth to do, but was nevertheless alertly prepared to do it.

I glanced up indifferently, and then, in a hop, skip, and jump, had reached the man's side and was pumping his right arm.

"Rufus Sedgwick! Of all men to run across in Paris! Let me introduce my good friend M. Lapierre, of the police."

I dragged the American adventurer across to the bench, where Lapierre stood staring in frank, amazement.

He told me, later on, that from my accounts of the exploits of Rufus Sedgwick he had pictured a gorilla-like creature, with abnormally long arms and a horseshoe jaw. Instead, he gazed into a pair of mild blue eyes, dreamy and poetic, yet shimmering with a serene intelligence and a tranquil self-confidence. A cauliflower ear alone struck a false note in Sedgwick's classic profile.

"Only arrived today," laughed my countryman. "Hadn't expected to fall into the hands of the police so promptly! I have a perfectly good alibi, however. Every dairy in America has installed one of those cursed electric churns. Buttermilk ruined! No more enticing little lumps of butter fat. On my way to Holland. If the Dutch have gone in for efficient dairying too, I'll jog on to Bulgaria."

We seated ourselves. Sedgwick refused one of Lapierre's favorite thin, black cigars, and waved aside my cigarette-case.

"The man who does the impossible!" quoted Lapierre. "What pleasure to encounter you!"

"Not quite that," protested Rufus Sedgwick. "I still recognize and avoid the mechanically impossible. I attempt nothing that violates the laws of physics — like lifting myself by my own bootstraps. Nor, in the present purely theoretical state of the fourth dimension, do I try to turn a rubber ball inside out without breaking the cover, or to project myself through a closed door."

"Still," Lapierre persisted, "our mutual friend has told me of even more marvelous feats."

"Most men beat themselves — I don't. I am controlled by my cerebrum, instead of my sympathetic nervous system."

"As *par exemple*?"

"Well," drawled Sedgwick, "it's a little like this. Here is a four-inch plank laid across a muddy street. No one has the slightest difficulty in crossing dry shod. Extend the planking, but twice as wide, around the summit of the Eiffel Tower, and ninety-out of a hundred would balk at it. Of the remainder, most would crawl around on hands and knees; two or three would lose their heads and jump off. Get the idea? I should jog around as serenely as when the plank was laid on the ground. Why not? Purely a matter of intelligent coordination."

"Granted," nodded Lapierre. "I myself could do that, although most unwillingly; but it does not clarify to me certain of the exploits monsieur your friend has related of you with such gusto."

"For instance?"

"Among so many notable feats, it would be invidious to choose," declared the little detective. "Still, for my own taste, that which he so drolly called 'Battle Royal' — wherein you invaded the resort of gunmen, and set them to mauling one another while you escaped by the window —"

"Oh, that!" deprecated Sedgwick, smothering a yawn. "The principle is the same, always. First, of course, I eliminate the chances of failure, one by one; and then, never allowing my nerves to assume the mastery, I just go ahead and do what I came to do. That is all there is to it."

"But M. Setchweek, if you will permit me! Brilliant as was the coup, it would be impossible here in Paris, in one of our Apache dens!"

Sedgwick frowned.

"Impossible? I abhor that word! In such a case as you suggest, I deny it."

Lapierre grinned, slowly wagging his head from side to side.

"It is that you do not comprehend. Our Apache — pardon me — has a certain verve which the criminal of your own country lacks. Modesty forbids that I should claim that he is a more desperate criminal, or even a more successful one, than your gunmen; but he thinks quicker."

"It would make no difference; I should adjust myself to his mental speed, and maintain the same relative advantage. That is all a matter of detail."

"Most men," said Lapierre, "require a little fraction of time to collect themselves upon awakening. With brutes, it is not so. Prod them, and instantly they are wide awake — teeth bared, claws unsheathed, every faculty alert for whatever may transpire. It is so with our Apaches, monsieur. The infinitesimal fraction of time, no matter how slight, that your gunmen required to adjust themselves to your surprise would be lacking to you in dealing similarly with our Apaches. Their minds are incapable of lofty flights; but within a narrow orbit, they move with unerring precision."

"Arguing about it gets us nowhere," Sedgwick crisply rejoined. "Make your proposition! My buttermilk quest can wait. Possibly your familiarity with this city may even help me to find some here?"

"Well, then, I would say that it would be impossible for monsieur to enter any one of a dozen Apache cabarets known to me, and some at least known to our friend; to insult the habitués there, and to escape unharmed, if indeed with your life. Of course, knowing your genius, I grant that you might kill several of them before they got you; but that would not matter to the rest."

"I will go unarmed, and I will not kill or even injure any one of them," stated Rufus Sedgwick. "I've nothing personal against them."

"I seem to recall," mused Lapierre, "that your stratagem was founded on extinguishing the lights. Your chances, naturally, in profound darkness —"

"I will not put out the lights. Like my friend Shakespeare, I have a prejudice against repetition. I pride myself upon originality and invention."

Lapierre beamed, and drew an ecstatic breath.

"Then, monsieur, I most assuredly repeat, you would find the stunt — is that your idiom? — impossible."

"You haven't been specific," objected the other. "Let me in turn outline the idea. You shall select the resort; you and our friend shall be present upon the evening when, having eliminated all chances of failure, I put this thing across. I will walk in, clad in evening clothes, insult in any way your knowledge of the breed suggests as most effective any Apache present; after which I will walk — not run out of the front door, and as soon thereafter as the distance permits, will join you two at a good restaurant, the dinner to be paid for by the loser."

Lapierre gazed upon him with respectful admiration.

"Your courage is above all praise," he said; "even though it be the courage of ignorance."

"Then let my ignorance at least furnish you an agreeable episode, and a good dinner," advised Rufus Sedgwick.

But Lapierre shook his head.

"Honesty forbids," he decided. "It would be to send you to certain mutilation, probable death; which would quite ruin both the occasion and the dinner."

"I will further stipulate," added Sedgwick, "that 1 shall emerge without a mark upon me, if that will ease your scruples."

Lapierre sighed.

"It is a sin to offer me this temptation at a period when time hangs idle upon my hands, and after having listened to so many eulogies of your methods; but — Lapierre is not a murderer!"

"Furthermore," his tormentor amiably continued, "a little side bet, if you like —"

"I am not a gambler," replied Lapierre.

"Now and again, among friends, I may risk a hundred francs, merely to add a tang of interest, but —"

"Five hundred to two hundred?" tempted Sedgwick.

Lapierre groaned.

"Doubled!" he breathed.

"Excellent!" cried our friend, drawing his wallet and pressing a thousand-franc note into my hand.

The detective protested courteously, but Sedgwick insisted.

"I am not so fatuous as to deny the possibility of an utterly unpredictable chance," he said. "Otherwise I should not bet with you upon a certainty. There is; one chance out of, let us say, ten thousand that I may make a slip. In such case, you might be subjected to regrettable delay in collecting from my heirs. This way saves bookkeeping."

Lapierre added his four hundred francs, and I scribbled a brief memorandum of the wager on one of my cards.

"The place I have in mind, then," said the detective, "is the Whited Sepulcher, No. II on the Rue Vinaigre, just off the Place Pigalle, on Montmartre. Here reigns a big, hairy one, who calls himself Gros-Nez — Big-Nose, in English. You cannot mistake him, for he has an enormous nose, a marvelous hairiness, and is of a bigness most unusual among the Apaches, who are a lean and undersized folk. But do not be deceived by his size; for he is like one cat. You shall, then, enter the Whited Sepulcher and advance to the royal table, halfway down the room; and here you shall pause to insult his majesty, Gros-Nez, who will infallibly be present after ten o'clock at night, unless he is on one of his forays. And then, walking out through the front door, as you have stated, you shall join us at the Petit Bleu, an excellent and entirely respectable restaurant just round the corner in the Place Pigalle. Is it not so?"

"It is so," Sedgwick amiably agreed. "And how shall I tread most effectually upon the pet corn of this — now — Big-Nose? My French is too academic, I fear, to penetrate his hairy head."

Lapierre considered for a moment. His face brightened.

"I have it! You shall stand before him, and cry, loud enough for all to hear, '*Je conspue les Apaches!*' That is, 'I spit upon the Apaches!'

Rufus Sedgwick carefully repeated the words until Lapierre agreed that his accent, if not perfect, was at least intelligible. I laughed outright to behold my dreamy, blue-eyed friend, his face gravely serious, murmuring over and over to the blossom-kissed air of the lovely old garden: "I spit upon the Apaches!" Lapierre, equally intense, leaned toward him as a solicitous teacher over a dull but faithful pupil.

"And for good measure," added Sedgwick, when the lesson was learned, "I'll tweak the big nose that gave the fellow his nickname."

Lapierre bowed as one salutes a hero about to go to a distinguished death.

"Then M. Setchweek, I, Lapierre, assure you that you will eat no dinner at the Petit Bleu, nor ever again see your thousand francs!"

But Sedgwick only laughed.

II.

During the next few days Rufus Sedgwick did not appear at the cafe where Lapierre and I lunched daily in the intervals of his assignments from the prefecture.

I understood, and explained, that my friend was engaged in a microscopic inspection of the Apache cabaret, the Whited Sepulcher, and its environment, in accordance with his custom before attempting the so-called impossible. In such cases, he could bring to bear an intellectual concentration no whit below that so powerfully evinced by Lapierre himself when occasion demanded.

"'In effect," said Lapierre, when three days had passed since the wager was made, "I am doing a thing most unprofessional. Compounding a felony, is it not? But I would not have you suppose that I am permitting our friend to endanger his life. I studied him well, that man, and I believe all that you have told me of his abilities. He is one in ten thousand. I am convinced that he can extricate himself from the Whited Sepulcher alive, though I am not able to see how; but not in the manner agreed upon. Certainly he has entered rashly upon an enterprise whose peculiar difficulties he cannot have foreseen; so I have arranged with some of my most trusted gendarmes to place themselves at my disposal. They will ask no questions, but will simply lurk in the neighborhood, separately, but all of them within sound of my whistle. In thirty seconds I can flood the room with intrepid agents. And do you, my friend, come armed, as of course I shall. We cannot save the gallant M. Setchweek from some rough handling, but I confidently expect to prevent anything serious."

"Nothing serious will happen to him," I laughed. "I know him, you see, and know his work."

"Another point," went on the detective, without heeding my comment. "I must beg of you to compliment me by the same degree of confidence that you feel in him. Place yourself in my hands. Make no move, do not reach for your automatic, or cry out, save as I direct. I soothe myself with the reflection that an ultimate good far beyond the thousand francs will come of this little adventure. It will give us an excuse we have long sought to clean up the Whited Sepulcher."

At this very moment, as Louis was filling our fragile coffee-cups, Rufus Sedgwick himself appeared and seated himself by our little table on the pave.

"I am all set for the big act tonight," he announced. "The table is engaged at the Petit Bleu for half past ten, and I shall breeze into the Apache place just ten minutes before that time. I have allowed four minutes for the act, five to walk from the Whited Sepulcher to our restaurant, and one minute leeway for emergencies."

Lapierre's eyes widened.

"You have allowed four minutes only, do I understand, to enter, tweak the big fellow's nose and insult him, and walk out again?"

"Well," Sedgwick argued, "this sort of thing moves right smartly, once it begins. I'm not looking for the slightest delay there; in fact, I shouldn't be a mite surprised if I gained a minute or so on my schedule."

Lapierre nodded.

"You have reason. If you get out at all, it is as likely to be within three minutes as three hours."

"That's how I looked at it. So, with the expectation of seeing you both at the time and place agreed, I'm off for a long walk in the Bois. Then a nice nap, and a taxi cab to Montmartre in the evening."

He shook hands cordially, refused a cup of coffee — "merely another variety of dope," he called it — and was gone.

III.

Stepping from the ill-lighted and sullen Rue Vinaigre into the sinister pallor of the Whited Sepulcher evoked the intended thrill. Its interior was white, even to the soiled floor of tiles, the flecked tables and chairs.

"Everything white," as Lapierre remarked, "except only the napkins!"

With that touch of the bizarre dear to the Montmartre quarter, the lights shone through pale green glass, imparting the cadaverous hue of death to the normally sallow and unwholesome faces with which the cabaret was well filled. Against this background a few luxuriant black beards stood out in artificial splendor. One's first impression was of a gathering of wax-works of noted criminals, endowed for the occasion with an uncanny life.

Most of the men, however, were clean-shaven, with creases running from nostrils to lips, and deep-set eyes gleaming in still and emotionless faces. The wide-vizored, baggy caps, the loose velveteen clothes, with dark shirts and long silk neckerchiefs, were the regulation Apache garb.

Otherwise, there was nothing to distinguish this from any one of scores of cheap *brasseries* to be found in all capitals of the world. Lapierre nodded to the patron as we entered, and received in return an oily smirk and a graceful bow, together with a penetrating though instantly veiled gleam from eyes old and wise and crafty.

No other notice was paid to us as we quietly made our way to a side table well down the room. No heads were raised or turned as we passed; the chatter, an almost Oriental staccato, neither rose nor fell. There was only this silent battery of eyes, all masking a furtive menace. Some of them were young and brilliant eyes of girls who had flowered amaz-

ingly in the *arron-dissement* from which most of them had never wandered farther a-field than for a rare holiday at St. Cloud or Versailles.
Others were old eyes, peering from mummified faces that had looked
upon street battles, and whose owners had crept forth in the dark to rob
the dead of all factions, huddled around the barricades.

One of the sloppy-looking waiters fetched us a couple of *bocks*,
and shuffled away. I glanced about the room.

There was a sprinkling of bibulous workmen, and, at one table, a
couple of self-conscious tourists, in tow of a smug guide, who was
ostentatiously pointing out imaginary celebrities, and lying fluently
about their biographies. These, however, were casuals amid the
Apaches.

Almost directly across from where we sat, my eyes were drawn to
the most striking figure in this congress of criminals. The amazing
width of his shoulders in a crowd where narrow shoulders and thin
chests were the rule, the unwholesome luxuriance of his oily locks and
his spade-shaped beard, set him apart; while a certain spurious nobility
of brow, a look of command, would have told me he was the king of this
underworld realm, even if Lapierre had not already so accurately
described Gros-Nez to me.

Above all other physical characteristics, his nose stood out — a
thing of horror; huge, bulbous, heavily veined. In this astonishing beak
was written the story of his life. It had been fashioned in the imperial
mold of the Romanesque, although its accretions had blurred the original design. Thickly sensual at the base, with spreading nostrils indic-
ative of uncurbed passions, its color by daylight, if daylight ever
illuminated it, must have been a royal purple; but, seen beneath the
sickly green incandescents, it bore the hue of a rotten apricot.

Big as the man was, his gestures were as swift and certain as those
of a spider.

"Were the prefect to say to me some fine day, 'Lapierre, send this
man to Cayenne! I would very gladly do so; but tweak that nose? Not
for ten times the thousand francs I stand to win from friend Setchweek
tonight!"

Lapierre's voice, coming softly from motionless lips, roused me from the horrified fascination with which I had been regarding Gros-Nez.

"And speaking of him, here he comes," he continued, a puzzled frown upon his brow. "Now, what the devil! I had not looked to see him in disguise! What can be the significance of that?"

To tell the truth, I should not have recognized Rufus Sedgwick. He wore a long, loose, and execrably cut raincoat, its collar turned up, and, pulled down over his ears, a flat, greasy cap. His face, as he entered, took on the moldy green imparted to one and all by the lights of the Whited Sepulcher, and a bedraggled, straggling mustache concealed his lips.

He stepped up to the proprietor's little counter and, to my astonishment, ordered and sipped a tiny glass of cognac.

Lapierre caught my look, and explained a trifle impatiently.

"But what else could he do? He enters. He gives to the room a final comprehensive survey. He must not attract attention. Were he to order, let us say, a vichy, the act, in this place, would at once focus the interest of the proprietor. Were he to stand there and drink nothing, it would attract the notice of the clients, who, as it is, have paid him far less attention than they did to us. And were he to call for buttermilk —"

Lapierre shrugged eloquently.

"But the disguise," he repeated, softly clicking his tongue. "I am vastly intrigued by that."

"I should think it obvious enough," I responded, a bit pompously. "Naturally, he does not wish to be followed for the rest of his natural life by Gros-Nez and his cutthroats, as he undoubtedly would be if he were recognizable."

Lapierre's frown did not vanish.

"Obvious indeed, my good friend; so obvious that it is not the reason at all!"

"Well — what then?"

He shook his head.

"If Papa Lapierre were the so great detective he is reputed to be, that disguise would be the clue to M. Setchweek's plan. From it he should at once deduce the scheme in its last detail. It must be that I grow old! 1 will add the thousand francs to my little hoard, and retire to the country and cultivate gooseberries."

"You still think he will fail in what he has undertaken?"

"It is an impossibility, as I have been at the pains to say already; and I do not believe in the impossible."

Rufus Sedgwick, having leisurely finished his little drop, and even smacked his lips over what must to his chaste stomach have been a frightful draft, sauntered down the room, his placid blue eyes seemingly engaged in no particular quest.

"I wonder if he has seen us," I muttered.

"He has seen everything, that man! He could close his eyes and name every one in this room, the number, their approximate ages, their features. He is a man after my own heart! Never before have I beheld one with whom I would so gladly work along my particular line."

Coming from one who loved to work alone, and who had never within my knowledge failed in a case he had undertaken, this was as fine a compliment as Sedgwick ever received.

"You have damned him with faint praise," Lapierre added.

And I had been almost ashamed of the warmth of my eulogies when on the subject of his exploits!

IV.

Working slowly and unostentatiously clown the room, Sedgwick had come at length to where Gros-Nez sat, deep in conversation with one of his cronies — a pockmarked Italian, a repulsive-looking fellow whose nose had been bitten off, possibly during a little domestic argument — such being the conjugal habit of the quarter.

Having in his unobtrusive way sifted thus far, he now paused, and stood almost at the elbow of Gros-Nez, leaning forward a trifle so as to bring his head more nearly on a level with that of the Apache leader, who did not at once glance up, but continued in parley with his sinister-looking companion.

I closely noted Sedgwick's poise, balanced lightly upon the balls of his feet, hands hanging loosely, every muscle relaxed, yet alert. One felt that were his nerves to be touched, they would sing like a perfectly tuned harp.

All men look their best when properly clad. Rufus Sedgwick looked best of all in a Turkish bath — where indeed I had first seen him; yet, even beneath his baggy raincoat, the man himself was revealed, as the old Greek sculptors revealed their gods beneath archaic draperies.

Suddenly Gros-Nez looked up, fixing a stare of inimitable insolence upon this stranger who had dared to invade his privacy. He even opened his mouth to speak; but the words were never uttered, for Rufus Sedgwick spoke first.

"*Je conspue les Apaches!* I spit upon you!"

His voice rang through the room. A sort of gasp hissed from table to table, and here and there men started to rise, hands darting to pocket or breast for the ever-ready knives. Gros-Nez, too, stirred his great bulk; and Sedgwick's open hand flickered out, his fingers seized firmly upon that atrocious beak, and gave it a violent yank!

A roar of astonishing volume dominated all the minor clatter in the Whited Sepulcher. The nose, I dare say, was sensitive. Gros-Nez was cruelly hurt, both physically and mentally, and even more astounded.

My perceptive powers seemed wondrously quickened. Without taking my eyes from the principals, I saw Lapierre's left hand take the police whistle from his waistcoat, while his right crept into the coat pocket where reposed his automatic. I beheld the patron lean far over his zinc counter, with starting eyeballs and out-thrust neck; and all up and down the long room the scrape of chairs sounded after Gros-Nez had uttered his appalling bellow.

Rufus Sedgwick, releasing the prisoned nose, with open palm thrust the big Apache violently back in his chair. Thus he gained a fraction of time. Then, instantly pivoting about, and seeming to gather impetus by spurning that distorted face, he was speeding toward the rear of the cabaret.

Even in the excitement, the thought flashed across my mind that he had lost his bet; for he was neither leaving by the front entrance, nor was he walking out! Lapierre's face showed no triumph, however, but merely an absorbed interest.

At the far end of the room stood a tall folding screen, which concealed the stairway leading to the kitchen below. Waiters were continually popping behind it or emerging from it.

I turned to my companion.

"Is there an exit for him below?"

"None. The Whited Sepulcher does not specialize in unguarded exits."

It took no time at all for Sedgwick to reach the screen, and to disappear around it. It seemed to me as if the squealing pack — led by Gros-Nez himself, who had rebounded from his chair like a ball — was not a half second behind.

The phlegmatic waiters flattened themselves, for the most part, against the walls. They were not paid to risk their skins in the frequent brawls of their place of employ. One apron-clad figure, coming from behind the screen at that moment, barely escaped being run down by the onrush of Apaches. For an instant it seemed that he would not be able to save his tray; but luck was with him, and he tacked carefully up the room, as nonchalantly as if, behind him, the blood of a gallant American was not being sought.

"The rat went below!" a voice cried.

By now, fifty Apaches were storming beneath our feet. Oaths, yells, the crash of china, and the clatter of pans and skillets came eloquently to us through the flooring.

I reached for my gun; but the little detective arrested the gesture with that quiet strength which always surprised me.

"Use your whistle, man!" I panted. "Are you going to let him be murdered down there?"

Lapierre did not so much as turn his head toward me, nor glance in the direction of the waiters' stairway; but, a slight frown upon his brow, sat hunched in his chair, his eyes fixed moodily upon the front of the house.

"It is, then, that M. Setchweek no longer retains your confidence?" he murmured.

"Confidence be damned!" I snarled, rising to my feet. "What chance has any human being down there with that pack of hyenas?"

"None — none whatever," he admitted. "Nor would he, of all men, expose himself to them. Come!" He rose from his chair, glancing at the watch on his wrist. "It is twenty-five minutes past ten; we have just time to keep our appointment at the Petit Bleu."

We walked toward the entrance, he silent and preoccupied, I punctuating each step with a hysterical protest.

The tables were two-thirds deserted. The proprietor had left his post to go below-stairs, and a sad-faced waiter was thriftily improving the opportunity by taking his place behind the counter and serving his fellows with the best cognac.

At the door, Lapierre turned impatiently at my final protest.

"My friend, M. Setchweek, awaits us for dinner," he told me. "I must beg of you to recollect that neither he nor Lapierre is an imbecile!"

After that I followed meekly enough, though without understanding, as the detective guided me at a smart pace down the Rue Vinaigre, through a narrow and forbidding alley, and so at length into the better-lighted Place Pigalle, where we entered the modest doorway of the spotless little restaurant known as the Petit Bleu.

A captain met us as soon as we crossed the threshold, and with a bow and smile led us through a *salle* well filled with entirely respectable guests, and on into a smaller and cozier room, where, at a corner table, sat Rufus Sedgwick, serene and unruffled, clad in his tuxedo, with uncreased and spotless linen.

V.

He smiled pleasantly as we approached, and pointed out two alleged American cocktails awaiting us.

"Took the liberty of ordering pressed ducks for dinner," he said. "Thought you two might not mind; and I have yet to see a real duck-press at work. The fowls are already on the turnspit."

We seated ourselves; and Lapierre immediately raised his glass to our friend.

"M. Setchweek, I salute you!" he cried, and emptied his glass, while I sat open-mouthed and staring like a silly owl. "It is that 1 grow old, as I told our good friend here. Your disguise should have otherwise made everything clear to me at once. It did so only in part; there are still points that are vague."

Sedgwick's eyes twinkled.

"As to what?" he inquired.

"As to about everything, so far as our friend here is concerned; for he is still confused to learn that you are not even now fighting the pack in the cellar of the Whited Sepulcher. As for myself, there is the question of time. I will confess it, I can grasp the raincoat and the apron, but the tray with its many plates!"

Lapierre elevated his shoulders and eyebrows in a gesture of surrender.

"The tray bothered me quite a bit," confessed Sedgwick. "After I had orientated the place thoroughly, from the seven different plans which were feasible I adopted the one that you saw me carry out." "I didn't!" I stated emphatically.

"Oh, yes, you did, you simply didn't realize it at the time, Lapierre here took it all in. As I was saying. I chose what seemed the least complicated plan. It really presented no difficulties except in the matter of the tray. As for time — there was plenty. None to spare, I'll admit; but when you are one jump ahead of the devil, and the deep sea is at your elbow, you simply make the most of that one jump."

"But to be certain of finding the tray, with its contents, undisturbed? Surely that required a confederate?" objected the detective.

"Bless you! I took no such chance as that. Highly unscientific! I had the tray all the time."

"You — *what*?" Lapierre stared at him with frank astonishment.

"I had it on a string around my neck; it hung flat under my loose coat. The glasses on it were trick affairs, fastened to the tray. Everybody was more or less excited. I counted on that, of course. For the same reason, I was sure that nobody would notice that there was a strange waiter present — not till afterward. The one detail that I had to leave to chance was that the proprietor himself might get wise as I passed out. It wouldn't really have mattered if he had; and as it broke, he had no eyes for me."

"You mean you were disguised as a waiter?" said I. "But how — when —"

"That loose coat," interrupted Sedgwick, "had only two buttons, and I had worked on them until I could shuck it off in one motion, which I did as soon as I gained the screen. Then with one hand I swept off my mustache, with the other my cap. I already wore my long apron, of course — not too clean — and as the tray hung around my neck, as I have said, I had only to tip it up, kick my raincoat into the corner where I had tossed my cap, and pass round the other end of the screen just as the gang arrived. The entire operation required, after considerable practice in my room, exactly three seconds; and I do not think a soul except Lapierre here recognized me as an intruder. The other waiters might have — they were cool enough — but they were too much interested in their free drinks. So I just snapped the string when I had walked the length of the room, set the tray on a table, passed outside, as agreed, removed my apron and chucked it away, and drew from a pocket my soft felt hat and my gloves. At this point, had I been working for a screen production, the director would have had me pause to light a cigarette, I suppose, according to the good old tradition. Just to help matters along, I had yelled, 'He's gone below!' while I was shucking off my coat behind; I got the *portier* at my hotel to teach me. I guess the boys understood my French, by the way they all piled down-stairs!"

"You cost the patron a pretty penny in breakage," I contributed, a bit lamely.

"He cost *me* a thousand francs," Lapierre grimaced.

"Only four hundred," corrected Rufus Sedgwick.

"One thousand!" insisted Lapierre. "Already, in my mind, I had profitably invested that wager in a little garden for the raising of gooseberries!"

The Fist in Pacifist

The first Monday in June has been "slap day" at Kingston since grass has grown on its campus, and water run from the old college pump.

At twilight on this day the juniors perch for the first time on the campus fence, silent and apprehensive. The dormitory windows are filled with underclassmen and their guests, but the campus is roped off. Presently a file of black-gowned seniors emerges from Dilworthy Hall — an edifice of vast antiquity, erected in the era of horse cars, gas street lamps, and gold toothpicks attached to watch chains — and makes for the trembling juniors. Here and there one is singled out for a hearty slap on the back, as one or the other of the senior societies thus signifies its choice.

Caestus is for the red-blooded, and gathers in the varsity stars; Book and Worm favors the bluestocking crowd, the scholars and orators; Domus Aurea seeks the silk stockings, the Prom chairman, the owner of the most expensive car, the men with registered great-grandparents.

All are desirable societies, with elaborate clubhouses and pretty pins; but Sarcophagus is the supreme goal of every Kingston man. Alone among the societies, it stands for no definite type of candidate. It would not be easy to explain just what it is that makes a junior eligible. It draws from all ranks, but never slaps more than ten men in one year. On two years, it found none worthy to enter the severe bronze portal of its windowless, granite house, the replica of a famous tomb. The following year, the first two men it slapped were the grandson of the President of these United States, and the son of Maggie, who for a quarter of

61

a century had been charwoman of one of the college dormitories.

Last year it gave the accolade to three: "Maude" Jillson, a youth with a Greek profile who had lived it down by proving that his corpuscles were of the right color; "Scab" Burke, whose father was president of one of the three great labor unions of the country, and "Pax" Rogers. They were fairly representative of the three social classes, were liked by the undergraduate body, and not unpopular with the faculty.

Before a candidate for Sarcophagus is deemed worthy to receive the sacred and esoteric rite of initiation within the hallowed tomb itself, he must undergo an ordeal in public. It is this feature which brings joy to town and gown alike. So severe are these tests of courage, moral and physical, that it is not uncommon to have a boy whose very marrow yearns for the right to wear the little gold and black enameled coffin which proclaims that he has won Kingston's rarest gift, weaken and collapse at the accomplishment of this preliminary requirement. So it fell out last year. Burke was commanded to write a passionate appeal for the open shop in industries, coupled with a violent attack upon union methods, and to publish this in a prominent newspaper under his own name, with the caption: "Labor Leader's Son Revolts."

After pacing the floor of his study all night long he balked at the barrier.

Maude Jillson was required to array himself in modish feminine attire — short skirt, rolled silk stockings, wig, sweet little toque, and with rouged cheeks and scented handkerchief to proceed at nigh noon to the most exclusive of the city's schools for young ladies, and make an earnest effort to enroll as a student.

Unlike Scab Burke, Jillson made heroic efforts to accomplish his task. He walked — as in a nightmare — to the iron gate of Miss Teller's seminary, and tripped up its flagged walk. When a scandalized gardener attempted to turn him back Maude knocked him flat with an unladylike fist, but not without having his wig disarranged, and one sleeve of his waist torn off, revealing a freckled, muscular arm. Proceeding up to the door he rang, and when the maid who answered his summons screamed and tried to close the door, he forced his way within.

Further details are matter of rumor. It is certain that Miss Teller, severe as an abbess, swept down upon him from the regions above, and that there were at the time two classes of girls passing through the hall, on their way to or from lectures. Whatever may have happened, Jillson presently emerged from Miss Teller's seminary, sped through the yard, and at the gate ran into an officer summoned by the gardener. Here he was arrested, and walked half a mile to the police station, followed by several hundred fellow students and citizens, all in a most genial mood.

He was bailed out and re-clothed, and the following morning paid a fine of twenty dollars for masquerading in woman's garb. Thus ended his effort to become a Sarcophagian.

The third man, Rogers, was called Pax because of his pacifist principles.

Pax was earning his way through college. At first as agent for a laundry, and for the past two years as operator of a dining club, he had managed to pay his bills and contribute to all the extra-curriculum subscriptions. He was a simon-pure pacifist who, nevertheless, held the love and esteem of the turbulent undergraduate body.

He was local president of the Intercollegiate Disarmament Society, and always occupied a seat on the platform at any meeting held in the interests of peace, tranquility and brotherly love. He had not been a draft evader, but had volunteered for the Red Cross before his country became involved, and had been decorated for bravery. He was a rangy, knobbly youth with big bones and whipcord sinews, obviously designed by nature for an ideal fullback; but because he positively refused to use the straight-arm or to try to put his opponents out every time he tackled, he was not regarded as a possibility for the varsity team. The stoicism with which he endured punishment from others, and a habit of never losing his head, made him a fine punching bag, however, and he had played for two years on the scrub, of which he was now captain.

Homely, awkward, loyal and clean, he was one of the best-loved men in Kingston, and his election to Sarcophagus pleased everybody.

For Rogers, a peculiarly obnoxious test was invented, a test which was of course based upon what was considered to be his one weakness.

It chanced that Battling Riley, the American middleweight champion, was scheduled the following week to meet a rugged New England fighter at Kingston in a ten-round, no decision go. Both because the champion was always a drawing card, and because Bimbo Dunn had been born in the city of Kingston, the bout was certain to be the big professional event of the year. Since no decisions were permitted by the State Commission, interest centered entirely in the Bimbo's chance of lasting out the ten rounds. The betting was two to one that Riley would put him away; and the local man's followers were staking much money on the short end.

For several days after he had been slapped Pax received no instructions. It was not until his two fellow candidates had failed to qualify that a secret emissary of Sarcophagus visited him in his room in old North Middle and confided to him the pleasing ordeal which, lest it come to the ears of Battling Riley, was not made public. Pax was commanded to enter the lobby of the Kingston Arms, the leading hotel at which Riley's manager had engaged the Presidential suite, and at an hour when the place was certain to be thronged with fans from both town and gown, was to approach the champion face to face and remark in clear, ringing tones: "Riley, you big hunk of cheese, you've got a streak of yellow as wide as the campus!" Nothing more. After that Rogers's time was his own, his little stunt accomplished. As Riley was known to be a particularly pompous, hot-tempered character, it was felt that a good time would be had by all. All, that is, but Pax!

A committee representing Sarcophagus would be present to see that their simple instructions were carried out; after which whatever might remain of Pax Rogers would also be carried out, the mystic rites performed over him, and he would be entitled to wear the little gold and black coffin which is rated by Kingston as a little higher than the V. C. or the D. S. M., and incomparably above all such trivial emblems as linked chains, squares and compasses, or the effigies of antlered beasts.

The peaceful one listened gravely and without comment to the utterances of the secret emissary. Such is the traditional etiquette of the occasion. When he had formally bowed him out, and, seated alone at his study table, gave the matter his prayerful thought, his first impulse was to renege. But his first thought was neither his last, nor his best. For reasons peculiar to himself, he was very greatly desirous of making Sarcophagus. It was a dazzling climax coveted by all true Kingstonians; but to Pax it meant compensation for much that he had missed.

Certain extra-curriculum activities were barred to him because of poverty. He could not bedeck himself in the glad scenery beguilefully set forth in the windows of the college haberdashers. He was unable to assume the staggering expense of seeing his girl through the gorgeous junior prom and its attendant festivities; and he suffered more over her disappointment than his own. Because of it he had not even gone stag. There were, in each year, other deprivations imposed upon him by a lean wallet; other sides of college life which he could never look back upon in riper years. Election to the haughtiest of the senior societies would go far to assuage his little griefs.

The fact that neither of the men slapped with him had qualified, that both had balked at the barrier, was an added incentive. Pride beckoned him on. After all — why not? He was under no obligation to sacrifice his principles. He would not be expected to fight Battling Riley! There would be no disgrace in running away from a champion pugilist, trained to the hour for his own specialty. The press would get the story, everybody would laugh over it, and the successful candidate would be applauded as a nervy chap who got his orders, and carried them out to the letter. Riley himself — reading the story — would harbor no resentment. It would be good advertising for him.

Of course he would resent the insult. He wouldn't be half a man if he didn't! And quite naturally he would attempt to wipe it out in gore. Pax Rogers's gore. But Pax felt certain that he could count upon a full second or two of stupefaction on Riley's part, that a stripling should dare address him thus. Doubtless, seeing him draw nigh, he would suppose him one among the hundreds of admirers who yearned to fawn upon him, bask in his presence, shake his hairy fist, and be able forever thereafter to say: "Battling Riley? Sure I know him!"

Then would come Pax's crude vituperation out of the mouth of a suckling. A gasp — a widening of eyes and then the annihilating fist. And during this gasp — this brief paralysis — Pax would drop his head and, seeking his opening — or making one — charge through the pop-eyed throng in the lobby, and flee as one striving for a touchdown.

Pax could run a hundred yards in eleven seconds flat, clad in mole-skins, sweater and cleated boots, with a football under one arm. He had never yet been tackled from behind. And never before had such an in-centive spurred him on as would be furnished by a berserk middle-weight three paces in the rear! Riley would not follow him very far. Pax knew the Kingston streets like a newsboy; but if worse came to worst, once in the suburbs, there was a good turnpike running clear to Man-hattan.

Pax smiled, shook hands with himself, and went to bed to dream of walking for miles and miles between double files of statesmen, athletes, soldiers and pretty girls, each of whom pointed to the gold and black enameled insignia of Sarcophagus, and sighed enviously if a man, or smiled dazzling if a maiden!

It was characteristic of him that having come to a decision he dis-missed the affair from his mind. The very next evening he accepted an invitation to speak at a meeting called to protest against the disgraceful exhibition between Battling Riley and the Bimbo. He was never in better form, and his remarks were applauded by battalions of old ladies and timid old gentlemen, and were quoted in full in the morning papers.

"Saddening as this blood-lust is, this inheritance of the old Roman Coliseum which leads two low-browed morons to pound each other for hire, they are respectable compared with the men and even, alas, women and boys who pay admission to witness a debasing spectacle! To call it 'the manly art' is an insult to intelligence. It is neither manly nor an art. If we cannot prevent this cruel and bloody exhibition, let us at least register our vigorous disapproval of that which rouses only the basest passions and helps postpone the day of brotherly love and uni-versal altruism."

Loud applause, and much waving of lavender-scented handker-chiefs rewarded the young collegian as he resumed his seat.

Battling Riley did not read of the meeting, and wouldn't have been interested if he had. There were nuts who couldn't see anything in a good scrap, he knew; and his press agent loved them like brothers and sisters. They were a great, free advertisement for him. Nor had the champion ever heard of Pax Rogers. He knew that there was a college in Kingston, and counted on its undergraduates to help swell the gate receipts. An old sparring partner of his had once taught boxing here, and once he had sold a bull pup to a Kingston graduate. That was all he knew about this particular institution.

At four o'clock the day after Pax's speech, the lobby of the Kingston Arms was comfortably filled with its own guests, a big squad of newspaper and camera men, local sporting characters, college youths, girls of the flapper type, and as many nondescripts as dared to pass the huge and haughty doorman of the great hotel.

It was not easy to get near the champion, who leaned against a pillar beside his manager, shaking hands in a bored manner with enthusiastic strangers, answering questions fired at him by zealous young reporters, smirking at the pretty girls who stood on the very tips of their smart little boots to get a glimpse of the fighting male.

Pax, strolling in at a quarter past the hour, decided to wait until the crowd thinned out a bit before getting his errand over with. He sank into a big leather chair, closely observed by three stern, silent men detailed by Sarcophagus to see that he omitted no detail.

Beside him sat a plump, nervous little sport who looked like a prosperous traveling agent. He tapped the young man on the arm.

"A fine-built feller, hey, mister? I betcha he wouldn't take no back talk from any man alive! Am I right?"

"Oh, I don't know," Pax responded listlessly.

Then, as a thought occurred to him, a twinkle came to his eyes.

"I'll bet I could walk right up to him now and call him a big cheese, and get away with it!"

"I got fifty says you ain't got the noive, mister!"

The little man dug suggestively in his pants' pocket.

Pax hesitated, and then he, too, fished his pockets. He had a trifle over ten dollars with him.

"Can I throw in my watch?" he asked.

"Lemme see it!"

The sport pried it open as a squirrel opens a nut, and squinted wisely into its inwards. "It ain't worth it, but just to be a sport, I'll let it go in for twenty dollars," he decided.

"Wait a minute, then." Pax rose, crossed over to a group of class-mates, and after a brief consultation, returned with twenty dollars.

"Here's my fifty, then," he said. "Who shall we get to hold it?"

The captain of the bellhops — invariably a sporting gentleman — was decided upon, as both knew him. He pocketed the money, together with Pax's watch.

"Here's where ya lose a timepiece, feller!" he said. "Nobody can call that bird outa his name and keep his health!"

"Oh, I don't know," Pax murmured.

The crowd was not quite so dense now. He rose, drew a deep breath, buttoned his coat, and began to work his way slowly toward the center of the lobby, where the gorgeously arrayed battler was "telling the world," from one corner of his wide, cruel mouth.

Let it not be thought that Pax was sustained by the gallant spirit of the martyr, the leader of forlorn hopes. The publicity, irked him, but he felt not the slightest tremor of fear. Riley, he had doped it out, would either deluge him with vulgar profanity, or he would reach for his jaw. He would be justified in doing either, or both;; but Pax would not remain to hear, or feel. He would be charging down the lobby toward Main Street. He would return to collect his bet on a more auspicious occasion!

The middleweight glanced apathetically at the youth who stood before him, and made ready to shake hands for the seven hundred and thirty-first time that day. But Pax did not tender his hand, nor did his face break out into the fawning smile of a fistic fan. Instead, he looked Riley square in the eyes, and in a high, clear voice like one reciting something carefully memorized he cried: "*Riley, you big hunk of cheese, you've got a streak of yellow as wide as our, campus!*"

The pugilist did not know what a campus was; but the rest of the sentence was perfectly clear to him, being garnished with the simple yet beautiful figures of speech he himself oft employed. A flicker of utter incredulity in his eyes was instantly quenched by simian rage.

Riley might be in nearly every conceivable respect inferior to Pax Rogers. But he possessed to the fullest degree one attribute that every successful fighter must have. He may be out of condition; a coward, both moral and physical; muscle-bound, yellow even; and still win many a fight. But this one quality he must have: his reaction time must be so infinitesimal that the response of the muscle must seem to coincide with, or even to precede, conscious thought.

It was so with Riley; and it made all the careful plans of Pax count for naught. For he did not curse nor strike, as his reply to the unthinkable insult resounded in this place of many ears. Instead, his left hand shot out with the speed of an adder's tongue, and gripped the boy's coat collar as an entomologist's tweezers seize upon a rare bug.

For the first time in his life Pax was scared — and dangerous! All scared animals are dangerous up to, and beyond, their utmost capacity to damage and hurt. And Pax Rogers's capacity was enormous and unplumbed. No man can play football for three years as a scrub and be anything but a tough bird.

Pax felt himself imprisoned, saw Riley's right fist clench, knew that at the very least a broken nose or jaw impended. He flung himself at Riley's feet, clutched him about the legs, upended him and stood him on his head.

No man, however hard or hollow his pan, is any the better for being dropped onto a floor composed of large squares of black and white marble. Riley came up, but he was groggy. He was full of fight, but could not have told his own name. Sheer instinct caused him to lash out at Rogers.

The crowd had closed in so that escape was cut off. Pax had to stay and defend himself. He did so in the only way he knew how. Instead of trying to parry the blows, he acted as if this were a football game, and Riley a plunging back. He left the floor in a clean, diving tackle that slammed Riley down so hard that his lungs became a vacuum. Then he picked him up, whirled him in the air as if he were a club, and felled three or four more or less innocent bystanders.

A surge of the crowd, a little opening, and Pax was through, head down, knees and elbows high. At the portal he met the huge doorman, who was coming in. The uniformed giant cascaded down the steps and halfway across the street before fetching up against a taxicab.

Pax Rogers made splendid time back to his room on the campus, and he did not leave it until the following morning, nor would he unlock to the persistent hammering of many visitors.

He always had a cup of coffee before chapel, at a little lunch wagon round the corner. No other student dreamed of doing better than making chapel sufficiently clad to pass muster. So Pax met no one he knew as he bought a morning paper, and walked to the lunch cart.

He found that Battling Riley and himself divided most of the front page between them, and about all of the sporting section. His own feat was played up in traditional style, and was about what he had expected, save that certain dramatic features made it of rather more interest than usual to the Kingston public. The genuine sensation was that Bimbo Dunn had not only stayed the limit with the champion, but had out-pointed him so far that he must have received the decision, had one been allowed!

For the first time that term Pax cut chapel this morning. He drank three cups of coffee before he had finished the paper he usually spent ten minutes on.

Then he remembered the single letter that he had found in the dormitory box; a cheap-looking envelope, bearing no return address, and with unfamiliar handwriting. He opened it and read:

Mr. Rogers:

I'm the man you made the bet with about you'd call Riley a big cheese. I'll be honest with you. I'm Bimbo Dunn's handler and I got a wrong steer that this here Riley hadn't done no training, and was a sick man. Well, when I see him there in the Kingston Arms I knew I was a sucker, because if he was a sick man I'm Sarah Bernhardt. So when you sat down and I see you was a husky guy I framed you to go in and start something with Riley and figured before he killed you maybe you'd anyhow mess him up a little so my man could stay the limit that night. Because, you see, I'd went and bet all the money I had, and a lot besides. Mister, I got to hand it to you! You done great. I made my pile all right when I thought I was a bankruptcy sure. And to show you I'm no piker enclose my check for five hundred fish which you earned it, besides save the life of

     Yours, (Signed) Bernie Rosoff.

Pax Rogers was still staring at the check in a dazed sort of way when a dignified young man tapped him on the shoulder.

"Be at the dread portals tonight at ten o'clock! Come alone, and wear your oldest clothes."

Thus spake Sarcophagus!

The Cipher

"Honor among crooks?" shrugged my friend, Lapierre, of the Paris Prefecture. "Where do you procure that stuff, *monsieur*?"

The little detective was naively vain of his command of American slang; just as I was of my French idioms. We were dining on the terrasse of a boulevard cafe, with the human tide making past us, and Lapierre watching it with the abstraction which characterized him during the interim of his activities; then he appeared positively absent-minded, and as far as possible from the astute observer he was when occupied.

We had been discussing the curious habits of the *apache*; that product of super-sophisticated cities who has arrived in his evolution at a point so similar in many respects to the aborigine that his title has been lifted bodily from the tribal designation of our most cruel and subtle Indians. Proving that extremes meet, so to say.

"Not only," continued Lapierre, fishing gravely for a morsel of ginger in his chutney bottle, "is the criminal forever being betrayed by his comrades, but I, Lapierre, tell you that he comes in time to be betrayed to an even greater extent by himself!"

Lapierre dislikes being quizzed. So I quietly floated a little brandy on my black coffee and ignited it, waiting for him to explain his theory in his own way.

A compact little man, stuffed tightly into his violet lapelled frock coat and with glossy silk hat perched on his black, curly hair, glanced keenly at us as he entered the cafe and bowed smilingly.

"Now, I wonder where I have seen that gentleman?" reflected Lapierre with a puzzled frown.

"It is *monsieur le Prefect*," I said.

"To be sure!" Lapierre nodded. There was probably no being whom he knew as well, or saw as often. Yet this singular detective, whose gift of physical and mental relaxation accounted in part for his ability to work brain and body to the last cell and the ultimate nerve, had not recognized him, because he had loosened the strings of his system. "*Ut laxis resonare fibris*" as the ancients put it. On occasion, he had been able to identify a criminal he had not seen for more than ten years, and who was elaborately disguised, aside from the ravages of time.

"I mean," pursued Lapierre, "that the criminal mind becomes so distorted that it can no longer rely upon those impulses which in normal beings are sane and wholesome. Like patriotism, generosity, courage. Me, I have seen notorious apaches, whose cunning had eluded our best efforts, fall like ripe fruit into our hands when stirred by emotions, for which we are tempted to give them credit. The soul, poisoned for years, reacts strangely under the unfamiliar stimuli of good intentions."

I sipped my *café gloria* and waited. Lapierre's ideas were often so novel that at first hearing my intelligence rejected them; but I invariably found that he could retrieve, from an inexhaustible store, some true story to exemplify them.

It was so now. Our dinner finished, our Havanas alight, he told me of Maxine, known to the police and among his associates as "Le Loup." It so clearly explains the singular self-betrayal of which Lapierre had been speaking, that I shall relate it, with no attempt to follow his idioms, since he spoke partly in French, partly in English, and with many expressions drawn from the *apache argot*, not all of which were comprehensible to me.

Maxine, whose patronym does not matter, since he himself did not know what it was, had grown up in that crooked nest of alleys that sprawls on the slopes of the Butte Montmartre. His education was comprised by the ability to read and write; aside from that he had learned all he knew running at large about the city.

He was a cruel boy, delighting in putting out the eyes of mongrel cats when he could catch them; stoning dogs, abusing children weaker than himself. He grew to be a big-boned, powerful fellow — God knows how, considering what he ate, that he lacked warm, dry clothing, slept as often as not in a market-stall or under one of the Seine bridges, and gathered and smoked with avidity the cigar and cigarette butts he fished from the gutters in front of restaurants.

He had never tasted water when it was possible to obtain wine or beer, and he crammed stray morsels of food into his ugly mouth with fingers which were the abiding place of every known species of germ and microbe. Yet he was never seriously ill, and although presenting the dead pallor and the drawn, haggard expression of the night-prowler and slum-dweller, was, as I have said, an exceptionally vigorous young fellow when he joined a unit of the great *apache* tribe — if we may so speak of the loosely organized body of thugs who infested certain *arrondissements* of Paris seldom venturing beyond their own territory except to make forays.

It is true that his strength was of the nervous, rather than of the muscular type, and that it was sustained to a considerable degree by stimulants and narcotics, so that by mid-age Maxine would naturally find himself prematurely broken and senile. But as few *apaches* do live beyond mid-age, this did not matter.

In a short time he possessed a creditable *dossier* at the prefecture, and the agents were looking for him for half a dozen infractions of the public peace, ranging from beating nearly to death and robbing an old, crippled news-vendor, to purse snatching and burglarious attempts. He lived well, his pockets never lacked a napoleon or two, and he maintained a ménage with a pretty little Breton girl, whom he had induced to rob her mistress, and who fled with him after the theft.

Things became so hot, in fact, that In order to save himself Maxine was forced to enlist in the Legion, the ultimate calamity, from the viewpoint of your *apache*, short of transportation or the guillotine; for he is miserable if obliged to dwell forty-eight hours away from the familiar effluvium of cities, and is even homesick in Paris when an exile from his own little congeries of cross streets.

Above all men he is insular, clinging like a fungus to his own cabarets, his own gang and his own convictions.

Maxine was sent to Algeria, where an Arab insurrection was in progress. Nothing could have been more repugnant to him. The flat, featureless wastes of sand, the searing heat of day followed by the peculiarly deadening chill of gorgeous moon-and-star-emblazoned nights, the rigid discipline, the utter lack of amusements, the impossibility of obtaining drugs or a sufficiency of wine, all aroused in him a sullen despondency.

He knew, from what he had heard and even seen, that they were lighting a people whose diabolical ingenuity in torture exceeded anything known to the depraved *apache* imagination. He had seen luckless pickets staked out on the sand with their eyelids sheared away, left to stare all clay long into the pitiless glare of the sun, until they mercifully went mad, and died.

Other things as bad he had observed. So that self-interest compelled him to relinquish any thoughts of escape, and to dwell in a close fellowship with his company, afraid to venture alone a few hundred yards beyond camp, since the children of the desert possessed a miraculous ability to conceal themselves on the very fringes of the encampment, where seemingly a lizard could not remain undetected, and where they lay patiently in wait for a straggler.

Wrapped in his blanket near a little fire of sticks and dried cacti, or doing sentry go in his turn, Maxine reflected bitterly on the hot and fetid little cabarets where he and Cosette had foregathered o' nights with their ilk, boasting of their latest exploits, drinking the fiery red wines of the patron, with dishes of hot snails or steaming tripe before them, and thin cigarettes wagging grotesquely from every under lip as the unspeakable badinage flew back and forth, so that it would seem that a signal service expert might understand their speech from the wigwagging of the *caporals*.

Or, he recalled dark nights when in some prim *bourgeois* villa he and his fellows had made a goodly haul, enough to live softly on for many days. Fights, too, he thought of with relish; of strangling rivals with his bare hands, gouging eyes in free-for-alls, wicked kicks of *la savate* — fights that satisfied, that filled the soul with peace, that had some intelligible cause; not the purposeless and dangerous warfare against lean tribesmen mounted on fleet horses or lumbering camels, a vile race to be sure, but one that only fools would give over the soft living of cities to seek out and destroy!

The wretched folly of it all brought tears to Maxine's little beady eyes. Sons of pigs! Fighting for La Patrie; and whatever could France do with this thrice accursed patch of sand once she had subdued it? Save for a few coconuts, it produced nothing!

It was different, of course, when they were relieved and sent back for a furlough in Algiers. True, it was not Paris, but at least it was a town. There were even *apaches* in it, men like himself, exiles of necessity, and whom he easily came to know.

Much wickedness they showed him, and for a time he forgot Paris, and Cosette — whom he had loaned to an utterer of false coin when he sought sanctuary in the Legion — and he made uncouth love to the outcast dancing girls, and learned to smoke hashish, and to swear in a bastard Arabic, and even took the stiffness out of his clever fingers by going through the pockets of a few rich tourists.

He became so reconciled to Algiers that the thought of returning to desert service was insupportable. So it was that one night, when the top sergeant was combing the dives to round up his choice company for an early march the following morn, he wept copiously, then became insolent, and when a volley of pungent abuse flowed easily from the grizzled old *sous-officier*'s tobacco-stained lips, he assaulted him murderously with a knife.

True, the sergeant recovered; but Maxine had done a plenty. He was given a swift and businesslike trial, dismissed from the service with dishonor, and sentenced to twenty years in Cayenne.

A little jest of the court that! For no convict had ever lived that long when transported to the isle of pepper.

It was then that Maxine's new friends in the Algerian underworld proved valuable. They rallied to prevent so manifest a miscarriage of justice, and presently the *apache* was smuggled out of prison, and aboard a felucca, and after devious wanderings that are a history in themselves, he found himself once more on the Butte Montmartre, wanted badly now, for murderously assaulting a superior officer, as well as for his numerous ancient and unsavory rascalities. He had never really pulled off anything big, so that the authorities were not spending much time or money hunting him down; they knew he would, if alive, return to his old haunts in time, and be gathered in.

Meanwhile he was home, a fact unknown to the police as yet, and safe enough so long as he kept under cover, and it was not made worthwhile for any of his companions to betray him.

He took back the slightly shop-worn Cosette and appeared once more in his set, quite the hero now and with a handkerchief knotted full of gold pieces he had somehow managed to scoop in on his zigzag return journey.

The napoleons ebbed slowly but surely, and Maxine perceived that he must presently replenish the store, despite the double risk. He was liable to arrest at sight, even if engaged in no illegal affair. He was deprived of that sound defense, the alibi. To be sure, he derived a certain reckless daring from the circumstances, since he would get nothing worse for cracking a safe than he would if identified at mass — were he ever to go to church!

He had, in short, arrived at that stage where he was an old sheep, to be hung but once.

He had changed somewhat, in outer guise. He was leaner and deeply tanned and bore a new scar on his left cheek, souvenir of an agreeable evening in a Port Said coffeehouse. *Messieurs* of the Service de l'Identite Judiciare would make short work of him, to be sure, were he picked up on suspicion; but, his beady eyes softened behind a pince-nez, he did not hesitate to wander about the boulevards during the evenings.

He never took Cosette with him, however, when faring forth beyond his own quarter, lest he be recognized through her. And he no longer attempted to practice sleight of hand upon prosperous *boulevardiers*. He simply kept eyes and ears open for possibilities.

His fingers often twitched to be in the pockets of carefree *flâneurs*, or to snare watches by their opulent fobs. But he kept them safe in his loose velveteen trouser-pockets. He saw, here and there, police agents in plain clothes, and carefully refrained from looking directly at them. He even tried to keep from thinking about them; he possessed enough rough-and-ready psychology to know that this frequently attracts the attention of the observed, as a magnet draws iron.

Little of interest escaped him. He had in full measure the Parisian greediness of the eye, the love of the passing show with its sudden glimpses of the fringe of tragedy, comedy and drama.

In general he confined his saunterings to the regions of the great restaurants, where is precipitated the wealth of the nations. Sooner or later a fragment of conversation, the shimmer of a necklace, the flicker of an eyelid would give him his cue.

Meanwhile, as he was nearly out of funds, could not pick and choose. Anything that promised a quick haul and an easy one would serve. And so, in due time, he took note of the good Herr Dienhardt, a big, rather sloppily dressed German who fed noisily on the *terrasse* of that very cafe where Lapierre and I were sitting — the Cafe de l'Orient.

Herr Deinhardt, he observed, was always to be found at a certain table at the hour of seven. Because he saw him repeatedly there, so that he became a feature of the expensive establishment, rather than because at first glance he seemed to offer any especial attractions, Maxine came to observe him with that alert attention he bestowed on every one he noticed at all.

And little by little the man became important in his eyes.

For one thing, he spent money freely. To be sure, he ate noodles, with a sort of clumsy dexterity, and incredible amounts of little red sausages ambushed in sauerkraut rather than any of the costly specialties for which the Orient's chef was renowned. But Maxine took note of the vintage of the champagne he drank, and the labels of the fat black cigars he smoked. His tips, too, were unusual for a middle-class German, which he seemed to be.

Above all, he was never without a flat, worn morocco case, which he kept between his feet while eating, where he could feel it, and which he tucked under his arm when he left. He never opened it, so far as Maxine could see, and it appeared not to be heavy. What did it contain?

Papers? Precious stones? Was Deinhardt a jewel merchant? Maxine never saw him enter a store.

His linen was always a few days behind the laundress, so to speak, and his frock coat, while of excellent quality, was wrinkled and even shiny. His watch was a big one set with a design picked out in small rubies and diamonds. It appeared to be a presentation affair.

Many people paused to chat with him, occasionally dining at his table. It was set too far back, near a potted palm at the entrance, for him to overhear any of the conversation; and Marine dared not cross the *terrasse*, where his shabby clothes would at once render him as conspicuous as a stage villain.

Herr Deinhardt's acquaintances were decidedly of the *haut ton*. There were spruce young officers, more than one of the old nobility, occasionally a musician from the opera, once a man whom Maxine recognized as the wealthiest Teutonic banker of Paris.

With one and all Deinhardt seemed to be on easy terms; if anything, his manner was a bit condescending. In his line, whatever that might be, he was a personage. Despite his uncouth appearance, he was of the elect. Evidently quite deaf, he had recourse to a gleaming ear-trumpet the size of a cornet, into whose concavity flowed much that Maxine would have given one of his last three napoleons to have overheard.

One night he loitered about until nine, and followed the German home. It was a longish walk, across the Seine and to a little brick house which stood in a fragment of what had once been the garden of an old Carmelite convent. In the crowded quarter, the tiny plot bore a fictitious air of spaciousness, and the house was well sheltered by masses of shrubbery behind its rusty iron fence.

Here the old fellow lodged then; for discreet inquiries at a student cabaret elicited the fact that its owner, a "decayed gentlewoman" whose family estate had been here for centuries, dwelt in what had been the porter's lodge, the last vestige of her ancestral pomp; and she occasionally let a room to some one unusually well vouched for.

Having heard this, Maxine made his plans to form acquaintance with Herr Deinhardt's morocco portfolio.

Nothing could have been simpler. Deinhardt himself was a methodical creature. Every evening between nine and nine thirty he passed through the gate in the rusty fence. The household consisted only of himself, *madame*, and one elderly serving woman, with a porter who pottered about the yard daytimes, and went home at dusk. The house itself was scarcely visible from the street, save in its upper stories. Maxine felt that the portfolio was as good as in his possession, and was solicitous only as to its contents.

The job seemed to be so simple that he needed no confederates. He therefore kept his own counsel, not even informing Cosette. She asked no questions, expecting merely that her man should produce a reasonable amount of money, not beat her too often, and allow her to lie in bed as long as she liked in the morning. Her household duties were sketchy, as they inhabited a single room and always ate outside.

Behold the excellent Maxine, then, on a reassuringly foggy night, lurking at the corner of the little old Carmelite plot at nine of the clock. He had fortified himself with a number of absinthes before crossing the Seine, and a genial glow possessed him. He had been careful not to enter any wine shop of the Latin Quarter, and to keep his long-vizored cap pulled well down over his eyes, having no desire to attract attention in the neighborhood, or to be identified by a possible witness if things went ill.

When he beheld his prey, bearing the familiar case, shamble up the curving gravel path and let himself into the little house, he lingered until a light in the left-hand upper room indicated his chamber, and then retired across the Seine, and spent an hour or two in a little groggery where he was unknown. At eleven thirty he made sure every one in the brick house would be asleep.

To obtain entrance, his ingenuity was not even taxed. He had' merely to decide whether to force a lower sash or to climb direct to the old German's room. He circled the yard, ghostly in the fog wraiths which drifted across it, like the spirits of amorous gentlefolk who had made it their rendezvous centuries before. No dog at large within the embracing iron fence gave warning. Echoes of the life of the quarter came to him very faintly, softened by the heavy air. There was no sound so loud as the snores which came through the carefully closed window on the German's chamber.

Maxine approached the darkened house and tested the rain-pipe which ran up the corner near the window he had designs on. It was ancient, but firm. Removing his shoes, and slinging them about his neck by the united laces, he began to swarm up the pipe, gripping it with his toes as he pulled himself up hand over hand.

On a level with the window, and two feet to one side, he clung to the pipe with one hand and reached out the other to try if the window were locked. It was not, and it opened both easily and noiselessly. To Maxine it seemed as if things were moving with sinister smoothness. It was all *too* perfect, *too* safe. Affairs that began so auspiciously had, within his experience, sometimes ended very badly.

In a moment his stockinged feet felt the floor, and he stood upright in the dark, listening to the Teutonic snores which alone broke the silence.

Drawing from his pocket an electric torch, he extended it sidewise at full length in his left hand before switching it on. Men had been known to feign slumber and to shoot with disconcerting accuracy at pocket-lights; and Maxine was taking no unnecessary chances. He did not focus directly toward the sleeper, but very gradually swept the ray toward the foot of the bed, and up its length. He beheld his victim, clad in a woolen nightgown and a nightcap, lying upon his back according to the habit of snorers, but with his face turned slightly away.

At this instant a series of appalling whoops resounded in the chamber. The noise resembled a siren, save that it was syncopated into brief double intervals.

He very nearly dropped his torch as his body stiffened into attention. Never in his life had he known such fear! Had the clamor greeted him before lighting the torch it is probable that he would have scrambled back through the window forthwith. As it chanced, his eyes turned instinctively in the direction of the din, and he beheld a ridiculously small cuckoo clock, before which a tiny bird was just finishing the twelfth and final call of midnight. Its body vibrated with the apparent effort and the contrast between its diminutive-ness and the volume of sound was grotesque beyond words. But it was also evident that the, noise came not from its throat, but from a great brass resonator which fairly dwarfed the clock.

Herr Deinhardt, being deaf, and yearning for some of the familiar noises his infirmity had deprived him of, had with typical German ingenuity availed himself of a super-cuckoo clock, which doubtless sounded in his dull ears with the mellow chirp of yore. Maxine had extinguished his torch almost instantly and now awaited in breathless anxiety any sign that Deinhardt had been awakened by an uproar that might well have been mistaken by the spirits of the old Carmelites for the final trump. But the snores continued, without losing a beat.

Again turning on his electricity, Maxine swept the room with a comprehensive look, hoping that the morocco case might not be hidden beneath the mattress. It was, as a matter of fact, lying in full view upon a little marble-topped center-table.

Scarcely had his fingers closed upon it than the snores of the old German ceased with a final gurgle, and as the *apache* once more switched off his torch, vague, uneasy stirrings indicated that the sleeper was awaking. The truth was, what the burglarious entrance and the vociferous cuckoo had been unable to accomplish was coming to pass from the open window. The damp, foggy air was entering the little chamber; and Deinhardt could not abide night air of any sort.

Without waiting to rifle pockets or rummage in closets, Maxine stole noiselessly to the window, succeeded in closing it after him, and slid down his rain-pipe to the ground. Two minutes later he was home-ward bound, with the portfolio buttoned under his jacket.

In the middle of the Pont Neuf, beneath an arc-lamp, he yielded to anxious curiosity. Seen from either direction, the bridge was unpeopled. A night-prowling hansom rattled down the Cite, a party of students sang behind him in the quarter, as they wandered home, united lest they fall.

Maxine's eyes fell, as did his jaw, upon a sheaf of foolscap, the sole contents of the morocco case. Riffling them in his fingers, each page presented a like aspect. They were covered with cabalistic symbols and figures, interspersed with dashes and exclamation points, such as:

1. e2-e4	I. E7-35
2. S g1-f3	2. S b8-c6
3. L f1-c4	3. L f8-c5
4. c2-c3	4. S g8-f6!
5. d2-d4	5. e5-d4:
6. c3-d4	6. L c5-b4+

And there were copious footnotes, numbered "a," "b," "c," *et cetera.*

These footnotes, written partly in German, partly in French, contained here and there a word that Maxine understood, although there was no consecutive sentence he was able to guess at. But "attack" he noted frequently; also "the adversary," "defense," "capture," "strong position," and "defeat."

In a flash of intuition, the *apache* saw everything. Herr Deinhardt was a spy! France was overrun with German secret agents; every one knew that! The rusty clothes, the evidence of funds, the conversations with French officers and the German banker, all fitted in as perfectly as fragments of a jigsaw picture. And he, Maxine, held in his hands a code which might well be worth millions of francs and thousands of lives to France!

It was here, on the deserted bridge at midnight, that he had his great inspiration. He held, secured by his own boldness and acumen, a secret the boasted *service de la sûrete*, his hereditary foes, had failed to secure. It would extend to him amnesty for the past. He pictured himself as a hero, with his name in the press. Doubtless they would give him a medal; possibly a pension! In any case, the slate would be wiped clean, and no longer need he hesitate to venture forth in the light of day, and without his detestable pince-nez.

It would be too much to claim that Maxine planned to reform, to become a worthy, tax-paying, wage-earning citizen; just as it would be too little to say that he was not moved by a certain left-handed impulse of patriotism.

Swiftly he thrust the precious case beneath his jacket again and hurried home.

The following day the prefecture received a singular caller, who insisted upon a private interview with one in high authority. "I am Maxine," he announced when the secretary had withdrawn, "known as the Wolf, and wanted by the police."

The *sous-prefect*, a pleasant-faced gentleman who could never have held down a desk-sergeant's job in an American city, politely requested him to seat himself before his flat-topped desk.

"*Pardon*, one moment, M. Maxine," said he, tendering his cigar-case, and offering a lighted match.

When the *apache*'s panatela was drawing, the official turned to a row of polished. speaking-tubes at his side, whistled through one of them, and uttered a few staccato words. In an incredibly short time there was brought to him a copy of the *dossier* of his visitor, which he seemed to absorb at a glance. He laid it aside and turned smilingly to Maxine.

"And now, *monsieur*, to what circumstance do we owe the courtesy of this visit? You have been good enough to save our department some trouble and expense!"

"I am expecting, *monsieur*, that the assistance I am in a position to oiler the government of my country will induce it to overtook any little irregularities in my past."

"*Vraiment*?" commented the *sous-prefect* non-committally.

Not without a certain *empressement*, Maxine drew forth the morocco case, opened it, and laid its contents upon the desk.

The official glanced rapidly over the pages, then looked up inquiringly at his caller.

"And may I ask what M. Maxine expects France to do with these?"

"Why, as you see, they are codes — German ciphers!"

"Indeed! And where did you chance upon them?"

"Last night I took them from the room of a German named Deinhardt, in a little house on the Rue du Bac."

Again the *sous-prefect* turned and whistled through another tube, and almost at once the *dossier* of Herr Deinhardt was spread before him.

"Why did you not inform the police, if you had reason to suspect Herr Deinhardt, rather than risk entering his room yourself without warrant?"

Maxine removed his cigar, opened his mouth, scratched an ear, and finally said: "I could not be certain, *monsieur*!"

"Naturally. All the more reason for relying upon our discretion! Attendez, Maxine; you entered this gentleman's room for purposes far removed from the safety of France. Then, finding these papers, which were of no value to yourself, the idea occurred to you to gain immunity by handing them over to us. Confess! Is it not so?"

Maxine said nothing.

"Even so," continued the official, in amiable and conversational tones, "why should you assume these papers to be of a suspicious nature?"

Maxine shrugged impatiently.'

"You can see for yourself," he growled. "What else can they be? They are quite meaningless otherwise, it is certain. Besides, he consorts with our officers, and a rich compatriot, and —"

The *sous-prefect* silenced him by a sign.

"*Monsieur*'s praiseworthy solicitude deserves a return. Permit me to supplement his knowledge of Herr Deinhardt by referring to the *dossier* before me. The gentleman, I learn, arrived in Paris on the eighteenth of the present month, detraining at the Gare du Nord at twenty-four minutes past noon. He sent his luggage direct to the room he had engaged, and with which *monsieur* is familiar. He then walked to the Cafe de l'Orient, and has, since his arrival, spent most of his time in one or the other of the two places."

The speaker paused and gazed curiously upon the man seated

before him. A quizzical smile played about his lips, and his eyes were cold, yet not without a hint of kindliness.

"Had Le Loup enlarged his horizon he might have learned that, beginning next week, a Masters' Chess Tourney is to be held at the cafe. Among the distinguished visitors who will compete in it is Herr Deinhardt, at present and for many years the German champion.

"These papers" — tapping the sheaf of purloined foolscap — "I shall hasten to restore to him, lest he do our national chivalry an injustice. He will perhaps suspect our own chess players of abstracting what I perceive to be most exhaustive variations of certain well-known openings which are bound to occur in the tournament, scored according to the German style. I note in particular a surprisingly ingenious defense against the favorite attack of our champion. Only a sense of honor prevents me from permitting him to profit by this!"

As Maxine stared at him, mouth agape and pallor struggling with his tan, the *sous-prefect* added: "I am not insensible of the motive that brought you here; if mixed, it was not utterly lacking in a patriotic impulse that your dossier would hardly lead me to credit you with possessing. This *dossier*, by the way, is incomplete; I observe that it does not contain a notation of your return to Paris. Your act enables our bureau to amend it to date. And I beg to assure you that I shall personally inform the magistrate that you gave yourself up voluntarily. That is always taken into account in mitigation of sentence!"

He pressed a button on his desk, and presently the door opened and there entered two stalwart agents.

Maxine le Loup had begun the first stage of his long deferred journey to Cayenne.

Robbing the Roost

As if in answer to his oratorical question, the black cat turned herself about within the space of a buckwheat cake, slid down the dormer window, and jumped lightly to the ledge below. A second later the tip of her tail waved a good-by to the man perched upon the chimney top.

Dion nodded thoughtfully. "An open window," he hazarded. "Servants' quarters, probably."

Even so his problem was hardly solved. Cool-headed and steady nerved as he was, there was little about the situation that appealed to him. Even to get down to the dormer meant a perilous slide on smooth tiles, and nature had not fashioned him like an India rubber feline!

There was nothing to be gained by remaining upon his perch, at any rate; and the prospect grew no pleasanter with reflection. He decided to enjoy one little smoke before making the attempt; searching for his cigarette case he made the disagreeable discovery that the arduous journey up the chimney throat had caused his automatic to fall from his coat pocket. Somewhere far below it lay buried in inches of soot in the baronial fireplace. Well, nothing would tempt him to repeat the trip to get it! After all the gat had done him no good when he had been made prisoner, and with luck he might liberate himself without resort to force or threat.

He finished his cigarette, tossed the stub in a long, flat arc over into the Rue Marboeuf, and, after removing his shoes and slinging them about his neck, let himself gingerly down the rough surface of the chimney. Clutching its sturdy sides he stood for a moment upon the ridgepole before slipping down upon his stomach; then, with fingers gripping the ridge, his feet extended downward toward the little dormer window, he began his perilous descent.

The tiles felt disquietingly slippery, the pitch was even steeper than it had seemed from above. He drew a long breath and let go. Flattened out on the tiles like a lizard, palms and feet spread to offer every possible resistance, it nevertheless seemed to him that he shot down with the speed of a toboggan. He had no time to wonder whether his aim had been correct, before he struck the narrow dormer; and, momentum carrying him along, his desperate fingers brought him to a stop only when both ankles already extended out and over the pavement, a hundred feet below.

It was more difficult, if less dangerous, to reach the window ledge than to slide down to the dormer itself. Only after a good deal of anxious planning and some violent contortions did he manage to make it, and to clutch the firm casement. Here he paused again, listening anxiously. From within came a gentle and reassuring snore. His moving-picture act had not disturbed the slumber of the person who inhabited the little attic room. Without further delay he let himself through the narrow opening and onto a bare floor.

Within it was pitch dark. Only the heavy breathing from one side gave him his orientation. He knew, at least, what to avoid! Moving in the opposite direction, and with infinite pains not to upset with foot or hand anything that might be loose and noise-making, he came at length to a door with a wooden button. It stood ajar, and it did not squeak as he opened it far enough to admit his body. He found himself in a large closet thickly hung with garments which exhaled a cheap perfume. Realizing that he was wasting time in a maid's clothes press he carefully retraced his steps and continued his circuit of the wall. Presently he came to another door locked on the inside; it took him some time to open this noiselessly. When he had done so he was in a bare hall. From the well far below a faint light crept up. Without hesitation he began descending its spiral stairway.

The doors leading off from the hall below were all closed, and neither light nor sound escaped from them. Here, he guessed, were the guest rooms of the mansion; and, with scarcely a look about, he kept on to the next landing.

Perhaps there is really a blind instinct which tells us when we are in an empty apartment; certainly Dion had felt this on the floor above. Here, while there was no actual noise, he sensed the nearness of human beings. No lights shone from the cracks beneath the doors; but at the far end of the hall, through ground glass, a very faint ray attracted his attention. Instead of proceeding downward through the house he glided toward this little patch of light and came presently to a large and very modern bathroom, evidently added within recent years, since it contained many novelties in the way of needle showers, pressed-glass tubs, electrical massage vibrators and curling tongs, medicine and lotion cabinets, luxuries not often to be had even in the best hotels on the Continent.

Dion closed and bolted the door. In a full-length mirror he had caught sight of himself and realized that, whatever the risk, he must wash up before venturing out on the streets. From head to foot he was smeared with soot, and his eyes stared through the greasy film. Only the palms of his hands remained white.

Hastily, yet without noise, he stripped off coat and cap, shaking them all over the immaculate floor tiles. Then, using a beautiful silver-mounted whisk brush, he dusted himself carefully, finishing by wiping his shoes on a linen towel bearing a hand-worked monogram in baby blue. Dropping another towel into a bowl to stifle the sound of the running water, he filled it and with plenty of soap changed himself from jet black to mild brunet. There was nothing he could do about his collar. Five minutes later, leaving the bathroom a frightful mess, he was back in the hall.

Again he changed his mind about continuing on down the stairs. At his left, as he turned from the bathroom, a heavy, white-paneled door stood ajar. He listened, but could hear no sound from within; but at this instant, from the room next beyond, a faint snore for the second time that night assailed his ears. There was about this one an indescribable gentility, a sort of feminine reserve, that convinced him that he was listening to little Madame Delyce. He tiptoed to her door and held his ear to the jamb. No further sound rewarded him; but through the keyhole there stole to him the faint, disturbing perfume that he had previously noted in her presence. Yes, it was unquestionably Madame Delyce who, serene in the belief that her prisoner was safely immured in a cellar built to withstand sieges, was here taking her virtuous repose.

Now a burning curiosity as to what might be in the adjoining room, carried Dion back to it against his better judgment. It might be madame's dressing room; in which case there might well be found in it some little souvenir of the occasion to be taken away and cherished! He tested the door, found that it hung on oiled pinions, and stole within.

There was no light whatever here; and he dared not use his pocket torch until he had made sure the chamber was untenanted. It took a good while to make the unfamiliar rounds, during which he discovered an empty bed, made up, and about a thousand large, heavy chairs, tables and cabinets, all with very sharp angles. When he had returned to his starting point he unhesitatingly flashed on his light and saw at once that he stood in the chamber of a gentleman of taste, and with the means to gratify it. Most welcome of all he beheld an open closet door which revealed a variety of suits upon their hangers.

Closing the door he bolted it. The pleasant thought came to him that he would here change from his ruined and sooty New York suit into something a little more modish and certainly much cleaner! And here, also, he should be able to find some clean linen.

He had little fear of being disturbed, and while he worked he took time to discriminate among the garments. Finally he stood clad in a beautiful shirt with pleated bosom, a French collar about which clung an exquisite gray-silk cravat, a frock suit, such as he had seen scores of times upon the boulevards and yearned for, and a top hat which could have been designed by none save a Parisian. With regret he found that the unknown gentleman's foot was quite a bit narrower than his own; and he was obliged to content himself with a renewed polishing of his boots, using a satin muffler he found. Some gold-mounted military brushes improved him further; and he felt that he could now move out of the house unmolested, so evidently correct and distinguished a gentleman being above suspicion!

Dion, after emptying his pockets and draping his discarded clothes carefully upon the hanger from which he had ravished the frock suit, now made a very rapid survey of the drawers in the room. This was work in which he was thoroughly proficient; and his industry was rewarded when, in a secret compartment of a writing cabinet, he found a neat packet of "*billets de banque*," the fascinating pink and yellow and blue bank notes of France. He skinned them over rapidly and saw that he had some five thousand francs. This was a delightful and unexpected balm to his feelings, and he freely forgave Madame Delyce for dropping him down the chute so unceremoniously. He found nothing else of value, but his dress shirt was fitted with a set of beautiful pearl cufflinks with studs to match. He wished that he might have found a revolver; but, as he cautiously slipped out into the hall once more, he felt that he had much to be thankful for!

In the vestibule there loomed up for the first time a possible obstacle to his peaceful departure. Upon a cushioned chair by the inner door, sound asleep, sat the ascetic-looking serving man who had admitted him. It was certain that he could not know that any one would be trying to get out; doubtless he was waiting up for the return of some belated inmate, possibly the gentleman whose clothes Dion was wearing. If he proved to be a light sleeper, it would be necessary to slam him with all due force on the point of his austere chin. Dion clenched his left hand in readiness for this lethal touch as he inched past him.

The fellow did not awaken, however; no further thrills attended Dion's departure. Two minutes later he was striding vigorously up the Rue Marboeuf toward the Champs Elysées, a figure which would rouse in any gendarme feelings of confidence and respect. It was not quite eleven when he reached his hotel; an hour almost provincial for an unattached young gentleman to betake himself to bed in Paris!

When the eyes of the clerk beheld his guest, who had gone out clad in a humble sack suit and cap, return quite the *boulevardier*, he betrayed the liveliest surprise, but his eyes had beheld stranger and far more exciting things. He bowed profoundly, as Dion passed his desk, and admired him exceedingly.

The little elevator was still clattering back to the landing when Dion put his key in the lock; as he flung it open he was nearly carried off his feet by the rush of some one hutlting out! They jammed the opening, swayed a moment, and then with a violent push Dion sent the stranger back into the room, found the switch beside the door, and threw on the lights. His eyes distended with surprise, as he found himself looking into the startled face of the debonair young man, the companion of the fair Madame Delyce.

Felix Rigaud seldom took an active part in the operations of the *Société Anonyme de la Haute Finance*. When he did so, it was usually to exercise his undoubted talents as a killer; on occasions, when the matter was very urgent and the homicide seemed essential to the welfare of the society, he would not hesitate to act.

Tonight he had broken his rule because he felt that none of his underlings could so completely undertake the task of finding the jewels, and especially the diamond necklace, whose capture by the impudent Yankee invader had so outraged the criminal band. He was perfectly certain that Dion would not carry them on his person when he visited the establishment on the Rue Marboeuf, even if he came at all. He was equally sure, since Dion was a stranger but newly arrived, that he would conceal them somewhere in his room.

When Madame Delyce had sprung the trap that landed Dion in the cellar, the leader had lost no time in setting out for his hotel. That the prisoner could escape did not even occur to him. There was no other entrance to the cellar than the opening in the floor, and that, even if it could be reached, was covered with a metal plate securely bolted. That the brick screen before the fireplace had been rather flimsily constructed he did not know, nor would he have been much concerned had he known. The possibility of worming one's way up the chimney, and then managing to descend from the steep-pitched roof, he would have dismissed with a shrug. No other fault was to be found with his logic, save that it was unsound!

It had been the simplest of matters to gain access to Dion's room.

Rigaud was a gentleman of engaging presence who could, and often had, wandered at will over public and private houses to which he had not been invited. No servant would dream of questioning him. His mere presence was a compliment. It had been ridiculously easy to pick the lock which was an old-fashioned one. There was not even an inside bolt; so the intruder had locked it with the same skeleton key that had opened it.

Dion himself, all unsuspicious that he had a visitor, had given Rigaud an instant's warning when he thrust his key into the lock. When Rigaud recognized him he was equally surprised to behold him at liberty, and to note that he was clad in one of his own well-tailored suits.

Although Rigaud was one of the most successful man-killers in France, he had not come here to add to the tally of his victims; but it took him only a second to recover his aplomb and to flash from its sheath his favorite weapon, a lithe, needle-pointed stiletto, which was not merely noiseless, but which made so tiny a puncture that a fatal wound would be followed by scarcely enough crimson stain to mark a handkerchief.

Keenly Dion regretted the loss of his automatic. The knife is not the weapon of the Anglo-Saxon, and, even had he been carrying one, his use of it would have been clumsy indeed in comparison to the finished Latin science with which Felix Rigaud handled his deadly eight inches of polished steel. It was doubtless fortunate for him that he did not have any knife at all!

Neither wasted any time in conversation. Rigaud moved first, leaping like a cat, his stiletto held in readiness to be thrust upward and into the softer part of Dion's body, where it would do the most good and run no risk of breaking off or being deflected by a rib. Such a blow is also more difficult to parry.

Dion gave ground, hands up in boxing fashion, his eyes never leaving the bright, almost merry ones of the killer. He had no plan, but he knew that, unless he managed to grasp the other's wrist or to knock him cold, he would probably within a few hours be lying at ease on the marble slab of the morgue, while a little stream of ice water played over him! Its counterpart in cold perspiration now began to gather upon his forehead and trickle down over his eyes.

Rigaud followed him up warily, feinting rapidly with his steel, seeking to confuse him and, upon the right opening, to finish the business with one deadly upward jab. In the end it was by no Anglo-Saxon science of sparring, but rather by his almost uncanny genius for sensing the psychology of a given situation, that scored for Dion the first point. Knowing well that a Frenchman will bear you no malice for attempting to murder him, yet will follow you for years to avenge an insult, the young American suddenly spat in the face of his would-be slayer.

The result was astonishing. With a scream of rage, losing completely his intelligent wariness, Felix Rigaud leaped in, lashing out with hands and feet at once, like an unbroken colt. Dion side-stepped and, as Rigaud lunged by, seized the beautiful silk hat, which still graced his head, and smashed it down over Rigaud's brow. The stiff brim scraped much good skin from his nose and remained firmly wedged about his chin, as he frantically sought to wrench it off. It was easy for Dion to tear the stiletto from Rigaud's fingers, and it would have been easier still for him to disable him, while Rigaud remained blinded; but Dion was too good a sportsman to do more than throw him and pinion his arms. He did not even do this, as it chanced; for, as he reached out to embrace him, a dry, emotionless voice sounded at his back:

"*Pattes en air!* Hands up!"

Whirling about, he saw that his door stood open, and was even then being closed by a little, elderly gentleman who stood regarding them, his mild eyes somewhat belied by a very short, ugly, blue gat which he held in one thin but steady hand. Dion stepped back, too surprised to speak, even as Rigaud managed to break the tough brim of his hat and tear it off, together with some more skin.

Just a flicker of recognition shone in Rigaud's eyes, as he beheld the little old gentleman with the automatic; but he joined Dion in raising his hands and silently waited for the visitor to speak.

Arnault Lapierre had at odd moments, while waiting for some crony to make a move over the chessboard, or while sipping a grenadine before his favorite boulevard cafe, devoted much thought to the young American who had been mysteriously visited by Rapin some days before. The situation puzzled him. Dion had attempted nothing against the peace or security of the Parisian populace; Lapierre had informed himself as to that, Rapin, too he had under more or less careful observation, since at the time he was engaged in no assignment for the *Service de la Sûreté*. But what were Dion's relations with the Paris underworld? Why had Rapin seemed to be angry when he left him?

Tonight, wandering more or less aimlessly about the vicinity, he had beheld something of greatest interest. Felix Rigaud, on whom the police had been able to "get" nothing as yet, but whose dossier, carefully preserved at the prefecture, was sufficiently lurid, was observed by Lapierre, while he was yet distant some quarter of a mile from Dion's hotel. The little man had followed him and without difficulty had traced him to Dion's room. Posting himself around the corner of the hall, some half dozen doors above, he had patiently waited developments.

When Dion himself returned and immediately upon entering his quarters went into action, the sound of the struggle warned Lapierre that it was time for somebody to look into the matter. The door of the room was not even locked, and he had entered just after Rigaud had been gloriously extinguished beneath his own modish hat.

Lapierre now motioned both men to be seated.

"Is it that I interrupt a rehearsal, *messieurs*?" he inquired gently. "Or am I fortunate in arriving in time to prevent a felony? You, Monsieur Dee-on" — he turned toward the young American — "are at least in your own castle. Is this visitor a burglar?"

The old inviolable law of the underworld forbids a crook to appeal to the police. He will bide his time and impose his own crude justice. Rigaud knew this as well as did Dion, and he was neither surprised nor especially grateful when the latter replied:

"On the contrary, sir this gentleman was visiting me by appointment, and we unfortunately lost our tempers."

Lapierre smiled dryly. "Was he not a little ahead of his appointment?"

Dion nodded. "That is true; or rather, I was a little late, having been — er — detained. I have no charges whatever to make. I regret that we have disturbed you!"

He looked keenly at Lapierre, wondering who he was. The hotel detective, possibly; perhaps a guest, alarmed by the row. In any case he felt that it would be wise to imprint his features and carriage upon that gallery he bore in his brain. It might be useful knowledge!

"What Monsieur Dee-on says is perfectly true," declared Rigaud. "With permission I will take leave, with my regrets that I for a moment forgot his eminent hospitality!"

"I think it a very good idea," Arnault Lapierre said. "Doubtless you will find that your young temper has cooled when you awake."

Making no further comment he turned and left the room. Rigaud followed upon his heels, with a salute to Dion, which abated nothing from the deadly hostility between them, but recognized one who had observed the code of their clan.

As soon as he had locked his door Dion hurriedly examined his secret hiding place in the leg of his brass bed. It was empty! Rigaud had had time to discover and remove all the jewels.

Dion at once went downstairs and requested from the sleepy clerk the package left earlier in the evening. He thrust it into his pocket and entered the half-filled café; and at a table apart he ordered a sirop and a siphon. While sipping his drink he examined the parcel and found his treasures intact.

The evening had not been wholly unprofitable, he reflected. True, he had lost the bulk of his jewels; but they represented the less valuable stones, and their disposal had caused him much worry. He still had the choice pieces; above all he had five thousand francs in cash, which he sorely needed. He had exchanged an indifferent suit for a very fine one, even though he had unhappily been obliged to ruin the hat. The pearl links and studs in his — or Rigaud's — shirt were worth something, too. And, not to be ignored he had scored a grand laugh on the *Société Anonyme*! He yawned contentedly.

"Wonder who the old bird was?" he asked himself. "Looked sort of innocent, but there was something about him — shucks! I'm going to call it a day."

Felix Rigaud, who knew perfectly well who the old gentleman was, did not dare return either to the pompous mansion on the Rue Marboeuf, nor to the quaint little home just off the Rue St. André des Arts. He felt sure that he would be followed, and he knew that Lapierre could "tail" him while remaining himself invisible. So he sought a nearby hotel and went to bed to toss about and speculate and rise to smoke innumerable cigarettes, and then attempt once more to get a little sleep.

Naturally he was anxious to find out just what had happened, how Dion had managed to escape, and what damage he might have done in the process. Meanwhile he consigned him to ten thousand devils, as he thought of the ignominy with which he had been treated. Dion had spat in his face, jammed his own hat over his face and taken most of the skin from his nose, and in general made him and all of them look like village orchard robbers rather than a handpicked organization of the craftiest minds in Europe!

He fell asleep, more than ever determined that, just as soon as possible, this upstart immigrant must be put out of the way. The mild annoyance he had felt at first had been transfused into a burning hatred. As a menace to them and because of his insolent contempt in flaunting them single-handed, he must die! And the hand of Felix Rigaud must be the one to deal the blow.

The Fascination of Guilt

"Do criminals feel remorse?" My friend, Arnault Lapierre, of the Paris police, repeated the question I asked him as we sipped our black coffee at a little marble-topped table on the Boul' Miche.

"Gratitude is said to be the lively sense of favors to come," he went on. "If we define remorse as a lively sense of retribution to follow — in this world or the next — why, then, yes; every criminal, excepting only moral idiots, does suffer from it. Not when things are going right — when their stratagems are succeeding, and youth and passion and money and glory are their bedfellows — but when nemesis tracks them down."

For some moments we observed in silence the endless procession which flowed past at our elbows — students, workmen, street urchins, professors of the Sorbonne, tourists. Suddenly Lapierre resumed.

"I am reminded," the old detective muttered absent-mindedly, "of the case of Félicien Descartes."

It was almost unprecedented for him to introduce the topic of his own activities. Usually I was obliged to angle with considerable inge-nuity, trying out all sorts of lures, and I was not always successful at that. To Lapierre, who utterly lacked the subjective viewpoint, a case, whether his own or not, was of interest solely as it illumined an abstruse phase of human nature.

I stealthily refilled the tiny coffee cups and waited.

Lapierre smiled whimsically.

"Consider, then! Papa Lapierre" — it was the custom of the man to refer to himself in the third person — "requires but little to make him happy. He is like an old dog, content with a sunny corner, a bone, and a few not too aggressive fleas. He spends his time with some idle good-for-naught like yourself, his world a little marble-topped table. He is forgotten. At the prefecture he is but a tradition to the keen young bloodhounds of the law.

"'Lapierre?' they say. 'Ah, yes, to be sure! The old one who was concerned with *l'affaire Roquelaure* — or was it the Pelletier case?'

"Then, one day, there comes to invade his moribund tranquility, to trample down the modest violets blooming upon his grave, a messenger. The prefect must see him — and at once! He sighs, comes back with a start to the realities, and finds himself once again entering that heavy archway off the Place Notre Dame, his steps echoing down the long granite corridors to the big room in which, as if in some previous existence, he has sat so many times before.

"Always it is the same. Monsieur the prefect greets Lapierre amiably, almost affectionately. He offers him one of his incredible cigars — fat, oily, full of the tropic sunshine, the rich, black loam and steaming vapors of Cuba, with a gold-and-vermilion band symbolizing the blood and treasure of old Spain.

"They light their cigars; Lapierre, not because he desires to do so; ah, no! — but because it is a manifest sin not to smoke a cigar costing two francs. For the rest, he will eat no luncheon that day; his old legs will wobble, his eyes will play him tricks.

"They chat of little nothings, gradually enveloping themselves in a thick and impenetrable cloud, like cuttlefish. And in due time, from, the prefect's cloud, a voice issues and tells Lapierre that Félicien Descartes has killed the beautiful woman he loved, and that justice must be done upon him.

"Yes, Descartes killed her — no doubt of that; and the intelligent agents have done their best; but clever Descartes had an alibi that the Holy Office itself could not have shaken.

"Lapierre asks the usual idle questions, because he is so stupefied by the aroma, the essential oils of his half-consumed cigar, that it is physically impossible that he should rise at this time. Descartes, then; had he no little weaknesses? Drink? Yes, Descartes drank; but, unfortunately, the more he imbibed, the more he shut up like the prudent clam. Women, then? He had avoided them since his crime. He had become, in fact, almost a woman-hater.

"The *dossier* is produced, the facts discussed. A crime passionel, my friend; in some ways the most difficult of all, in others the simplest. Simple, because the great elemental impulses are alone involved; complex, because the assassin is at the time not himself. Swayed by blind rage or jealousy, strangely mingled with a terrible love, he does not act according to his normal character.

"At length that appalling cigar has burned down to its nicotine-soaked butt. Lapierre reverently lays it aside, its firm, crisp ash unbroken, and essays to depart. At need he can press the button which will set in motion the stupendous and well-oiled mechanism of the Paris police system, the finest in the world. Outside in the corridor he pauses to light one of his own thin black cigars — as an antidote to that terrible Havana of the prefect's.

"Thus, my old one, I undertook the commission to convict Félicien Descartes," said Lapierre, speaking of himself now in the first person. "With no plan, no special instructions, only the bare details — and facing that alibi which had baffled our *flics*. And what think you I did, first of all?"

I shook my head.

II.

"I visited the small apartment where had lived Céleste Nivelle, and where she had so dreadfully died," the old detective resumed after a pause. "Our agents, my friend, are of an intelligence. One may rely upon them! And so it was that I knew the room would have been left by them in the precise condition in which they found it. Where a chair had fallen, there it would lie. Where blood bespattered the walls, no hand would have washed it clean. They had simply locked and sealed the door and gone away.

"It was mid-afternoon when I found myself in front of the block on the Boulevard Haussmann, fronting a new park, in which Celeste

Nivelle had been installed.

Her suite was in the *entresol*, consisting of a pleasant salon over-looking the park, a bedchamber, and an immaculate kitchenette. Her maid, Lilas, did not sleep on the premises, but came each morning to prepare her mistress's coffee, fetching with her a basket of white rolls from the bakery.

"The sunlight flooded through the windows of the salon when I raised the Venetian blinds, after closing and locking the door. It was within this room that the girl had been slashed to ribbons by her infuri-ated lover, for no reason which the police were able to discover. The maid, Lilas, insisted that there was no other man involved, and that nothing beyond the usual lovers' tiffs had ever marred their life. She may have been keeping something back, but after scouring the resorts and interrogating the gay irresponsibles amid whom they passed their time, no light was thrown upon the motive for the crime; nor did a methodical search of their effects add anything. As to the reasons for definitely identifying Descartes as the assassin, even I, Lapierre, did not know; I was satisfied, as always, to accept the word of the prefect and trust the efficiency of our agents. It was my part to connect Descartes with the murder.

"I walked about the room, letting its atmosphere sink in. Nothing, as I have told you, had been disturbed. At this very moment the sun was caressing a warm-toned etching of a 'Weeping Magdalen,' hanging over Céleste's writing-cabinet The walls were papered in dull gold, fig-ured with tulips of a deeper tone. There were a dozen good pictures on them as well as an antique mirror with brass sconces. In the sconces stood cream-colored wax candles which had never been lighted. The woodwork was enameled in ivory tones; a beautiful buff rug some three yards square, with a contrasting Persian-blue figure, a great hanging lamp of copper with a shade of amber glass, and draperies of pale-lemon silk, maintained the key in which the color scheme had been pitched by some clever decorator, or, possibly, by *mademoiselle* herself.

"The rug was rumpled and stained with blood. So also was the wall, at one side; and here was the print of a small hand, in blood, the tapering fingers outspread, the clearness of the impression indicating that it had been flung out forcibly, seeking support. I took note of every detail; for" — Lapierre smiled — "though I am so absent-minded that my pockets have been picked and that I offend my good friends by passing them on the street without recognition, I am also on occasion one whom nothing whatever escapes.'"

I had been told that once Lapierre, elaborately arrayed, sat at such a table as the one across which we were talking now, absorbed in his reveries, and that, chancing to observe a little procession passing by, and idly inquiring of the waiter what might be its occasion, he was told that it was the wedding party of a famous detective, Lapierre, who was taking to himself a bride in the nearby church of St. Augustin. As a matter of fact, the little party was returning from the church, the groom having failed to materialize!

That was the nearest Lapierre ever came to matrimony. Yet this man, when he chose to concentrate, as on one of his cases, became an implacable mind, coldly and infallibly sifting the evidence brought to him by senses which missed nothing. At such times even his power of smell seemed to become like that of a feral creature.

"Irrelevant details?" he had once remarked. "There are none!"

"Alone within this still room, the scene of much former joyousness, I discarded my personality as a man discards his coat," he continued. "I became Félicien Descartes, moved by blinding passion. I leaped upon the lovely girl about whom my world had been constructed; I rejoiced to feel the soft flesh yield to my iron fingers and to behold the widening pupils of the anguished eyes she turned upon me. I felt as Félicien felt when the soul of her drained off through many cruel gashes!

"Reason crept back, and I made my plans to escape. Had any one heard our struggle? Was my face marked? Should I leave at once, or wait till dark? For — so the police said — it was at about this hour that Celeste met her death.

"Again, I put myself in the place of the girl. In her place? Nay, *I was the girl*! Young, beautiful, amorous, living a sheltered and perfumed existence, at twenty-two I looked into the grinning face of Death, and knew that I must leave it all; that in five minutes — or three — I should be a thing to shudder at, even as I had often shrunk from a dead cat lying in the gutter. Desperately I struggled to avert this horror, this unprepared-for call to yield my tender body and my greedy youth!

"Do you believe, as I sometimes do, that even to inanimate things there attaches an impalpable essence of the personalities which have been associated with them? In a corner of that room was a broken *chaise longue* — a lovely thing of marquetry which had once belonged to the Pompadour, and had for generations passed from hand to hand, always associated with love and kisses. It had come to ruin, fittingly enough; for upon it were found the poor crumpled lace and blood, the cold, white flesh; and wide, terrified eyes that had been Céleste Nivelle.

"Laugh, I pray you, if it please you; I shall take no offense; but" — Lapierre leaned over the table, his gaze fixed upon me, and continued his narrative in a whisper — "I became that pretty toy, that broken *chaise longue*. I felt upon my cunningly inlaid fabric the devastating impact of the victim of Descartes. Her blood soaked into my dainty brocade. We perished together!

III.

"I was roused by one of those curious happenings which are so eagerly seized upon by the superstitious. Upon the mantel stood a foolish little Swiss clock — one of those from whose rustic interior a brown cuckoo emerges to announce the hour. Suddenly — jarred, as I believe, by a heavy truck which rumbled past — the flimsy door of the clock opened, and the tiny inmate crept forth with a dry rustle. Halfway out it stopped and opened its beak, but uttered no sound. After a moment it withdrew, and the door closed after it. The mechanism had run down, save for this final modicum of energy, set in action by the jarring; but the effect was precisely as if the futile toy had tried to convey some message. Imbued as I was with the tragedy upon which I had been concentrating, and taking place in the fast-gathering dusk, the effect was weird and even sinister."

Lapierre paused and sighed. He lighted one of his thin cigars.

"When I left that room I knew it as if I had lived within it for years. The other rooms, the chamber and the kitchenette, I merely glanced over. And the following day I set to work to reconstruct that little salon. Not, you understand, to repair it, nor to put it approximately where it was when, upon that fatal afternoon, Félicien Descartes entered it for the last time; but to put it *exactly* as it then was.

"First of all, there was a roll of paper to be replaced. With some trouble I found the decorator from whom it had been purchased years before; but when matched it proved a little brighter than that which had hung there so long. The difference was slight, it is true; but when Descartes entered the reconstructed room his eyes would unerringly be led to that very section and might note its lighter hue. Therefore, the entire room must be repapered.

"This was not so simple; for there was but a single roll of that pattern left in stock, and none had been printed for several years. To arrange to have a special lot made up from the old blocks, most fortunately preserved, entailed time and trouble; and when the job was done it proved as expensive as if the room had been draped with damask.

"Next, there was the matter of the *chaise longue*. It might be repaired, but never so that a close inspection would not have revealed the patchwork. Again, this was a thing which would be certain to draw Descartes' gaze with a terrible fascination. So, the best maker of antique cabinets in Paris was employed to construct an exact duplicate — exact, you understand, to the very dents and scratches of the original, including a fragment of missing ebony in the inlay.

"The rug yielded readily to the naphtha process. Presently, then, the salon stood precisely as upon that day when its dainty interior was desecrated by so terrible a storm of passion and crime.

"After all, it was a cat which proved more troublesome than all else together — a huge yellow animal answering to the name of Henrique. I assure you that before I found one that satisfied the critical eyes of Lilas, who was by now in my pay, I knew half the animal shops in Paris! I was a connoisseur in the indescribable odors, the raucous cries, the forlorn attempts to make friends, of every species of pet which can exist in our climate. And when we finally selected a cat, he was not perfect; he had a long tail — a plume of magnificence, which he managed with dignity and grace. Poor Henrique, who had fled from the death-scene of his mistress, and had never returned, was bobtailed, a genuine Manx. We sacrificed all but two inches of our cat's tail, and when his feelings were somewhat assuaged, Lilas undertook to teach him his new name. Many times a day would she call, 'Henrique! Come thou here, *mon enfant!*' and offer him the reward of a scrap of raw kidney; till at length he accepted his new name and came running whenever he was called.

"Now, having done all that pains and ingenuity could suggest to restore old conditions, I took a little vacation and buried myself in an old Norman seaport for a week or two. I wished to meditate in its dull and sleepy air. Also, Félicien Descartes was a Norman. He possessed the shrewdness of the peasant, overlaid with the sophistication of the city; not an easy character to penetrate, you will perceive. Among his sort of folk, I felt that I could study to advantage the instincts which move them; for all Normans run pretty true to type. Were they superstitious? Religious? Brave? Stolid? I purposed to see for myself.

"I had no routine work to do, no reports to hand in, no colloquies with my superior. As you know, my friend, I work along individual lines, unhampered by the official red tape of my confreres. I might have ended my days in this old seaport of the Conqueror, and no one would have interfered; but in ten days I was back in Paris. We soon yearn for the boulevards, we true Parisians, and our own little table on the pavé! Besides, my plan was by now matured.

"Lest you should think that I am boastful, let me say that I should have failed, or at least that this plan would have had to be abandoned, but for the cooperation of a most remarkable woman.

"*Monsieur,* in all the world there is nothing so implacable as a wronged woman. A man may feel a fiercer rage at the moment; but he is turned from his purpose by many things. A woman never forgets!

"It was Julie, the sister of the dead Celeste, to whom I went for assistance and unfolded my plan. She was *femme exquise,* lovely like her sister, though a year or two older. Indeed, when the hairdresser and modiste had done with her she was Celeste herself, so Lilas admitted, I, of course, had never seen the murdered woman.

"There was one detail lacking; and it was in supplying this that Julie proved the depth of her hatred for Descartes. Conceive a really beautiful woman who will permit a surgeon to mar her face with a scar! For Céleste had borne one across her right cheek, the result of an accident in girlhood; not, to be sure, very noticeable, but nevertheless a blemish. So Julie must needs be cut, and healed; and even then she would have no assurance that it would be of any utility. Yet, merely on the chance that it might help bring to justice this man upon whom she had never set eyes, she submitted willingly and even joyously to the little operation, performed by one of our discreet police surgeons. Then, under Lilas's tuition, since she had seen her sister but rarely during the past few years, she studied the dead Céleste's tricks of voice and gesture, hummed her favorite ballads, worked like a true *artiste* perfecting herself in an important role.

"Meanwhile, I had seen Félicien Descartes once or twice and one of our agents had kept him under surveillance. The agent, posing as rather a dull fellow addicted to liquor, had easily enough made and held his acquaintance. I had observed him across a cafe, or from a theater gallery, but with far less attention than I customarily bestow. I had read the reports, and felt that I knew as much as I needed to know about this thick-bodied, square-headed, rather surly young fellow, who was drinking steadily, never retiring until dawn stained the sky, who neglected his meals for long periods and then ate voraciously. He was not happy, this man; but he held an iron grip upon himself, and never did his tongue prove an unruly member.

IV.

"At length, all being in readiness, I passed the word to the agent. A long evening of drinking, that Félicien Descartes might arrive at that state where a clear memory of the past few hours was beyond probability; and then, in the last glass, the pinch of powder carried by our agent."

Again Lapierre paused, his head sunk forward, his thin black cigar drooping from his lips. He sighed and looked up.

"Félicien Descartes awakened in the room of which every detail must have been burned into his memory. Save for the bed in which he lay, which had been moved from the adjoining chamber, all was as he knew it before the tragedy.

"About his forehead was bound a thick linen bandage. His head ached splittingly; he tried vainly to recall what had happened to him.

"By his side, solicitude in her eyes, a smile of love and sympathy upon her lips, sat a beautiful girl, busy about some glasses and vials upon the little stand which was by the bed. The man's lips noiselessly formed the word 'Céleste.'

"The girl leaned over him, placing a cool hand upon his cheek. At that instant, from the door leading to the hall, there entered, with brisk, professional air, a man bearing a physician's bag, who advanced to the bedside. It was I — Lapierre, 'doctor despite himself,' is it not?

"'Oh, doctor, I think he is better! There is a different look in his eyes!' the girl cried, tears rising to her eyes.

"'Well, well!' I replied, bending over the patient. 'We shall see what we shall see!' I opened my bag — a very proper bag, borrowed from the police surgeon, and packed with all manner of things the use of which I could but conjecture.

"I found what I was after — a little oral thermometer, which I thrust, with an air, into my patient's mouth. After a moment I withdrew and frowningly observed it.

"'You have reason, *madame*,' I reassured her. 'The fever has abated itself. The crisis is passed. I can promise you that your husband will live!'

"I could indeed have told almost precisely how long he would live!

"Hungrily, Descartes scanned the features of the girl bending above him. He could not, you understand, see too clearly — a drop or so of atropine had arranged that while he slept. He raised his hand to her face. His fingers sought — and found — the tiny scar upon it.

"The girl endured his touch without flinching; but she gently raised her head and called, 'Oh, Henrique! Come and see the master!' There entered, from the left rear, and quite theatrically, the great yellow cat, who sat expectantly at her feet, licking his chops. But there was no delectable morsel of kidney today! Poor Henrique had played out his little part.

"The eyes of Descartes passed from object to object in the room; first, to that part of the wall where had been the bloody print of the little hand, then over the clean rug, to finger upon the chaise lounge. From its cage emerged the tiny brown bird. 'Cocu!' it chirped, nine times, and retired.

"'*Eh bien! Qu'est-ce que tu nous chantes*? What tune singest thou?' muttered Descartes.

"I took out a pad of prescription blanks and began to write — not remedies, however, but in shorthand, everything that Descartes said.

"'You have been so very, very ill, *p'tit maître*,' crooned the girl. 'One feared you would have died. A fall, we suppose; or possibly a blow. Strangers left you at our door unconscious. This was ten long days ago!'

"A cunning look flickered across the man's heavy features.

"'Let me then see the newspaper,' he said.

"The girl called aloud: '*Lilas, les nouvelles du jour!*'

"Lilas entered, curtsied to her master, and showed her white teeth. In her hand she bore a fresh newspaper of the tenth day after Céleste Nivelle's murder. Descartes seized it and managed to focus his eyes upon it to read the date.

"'Name of God, but I have had a most ghastly dream!' Once more he fastened his eyes upon the girl's features.

"'Yes — yes — we know,' she soothed him. 'You were in a delirium; but you must forget it now and not exert yourself to talk.'

"Descartes stirred restlessly. His great hands plucked at the silk coverlet. 'I thought I had killed you, Céleste, *chérie*!' he whispered.

"The girl laughed softly. 'I am not so easily handled! Me, I am of a strength and suppleness.'

"'*Dieu*, do I not know it? I thought — in my dream — that you would never die!'

"'*Mais, mon choux*, silly one that thou art, who wouldst not harm poor Henrique here, why shouldst thou kill me, even in a dream?'

"He wagged his head upon its pillow. 'Oh — the usual stupid lovers' quarrel; beginning with nothing and ending in blood — blood everywhere! I had been drinking — naturally —' He paused, closing his eyes. After a moment he went on: 'It was so real — so horribly real! Each detail! Not like any dream I ever had before. *I thought I was damned!* And now — now I can enter a church, and the fumes of incense will not strangle me! I can kneel before God — and, sinner as I am, He will not smite me dead for sacrilege!'

"The girl patted his hand, as one humoring a child. 'And they condemned you to death, *mon brave*, in your dream?'

"'No! I was too clever for them; even in my dream I was not to be trapped. I sold my big ring to old Baltasar, the Jew, and gave the money to crooked Maître Richard to buy me an alibi —'

"He stopped abruptly and gazed at his hands, spread before him on the soft coverlet. '*Où donc?* Where is it — my diamond?' His voice sounded harsh and flat.

"The girl hesitated. Of course I had a reply ready in case he had noticed at first that the big yellow stone he always wore upon his middle finger was missing; but now it could make no difference. In the relief from the terrible mental strain under which he had held himself taut during all these weeks, he had told me more than I had dared to hope for.

"I stepped forward, at the same time beckoning to two agents who were waiting within the inner chamber.

"'Old Baltasar shall recover it for us, *monsieur*,' I said."

"He turned a dreadful visage upon me, and, without speaking, pointed to the girl, who had risen and was staring down at him with a gloating ferocity.

"'Mile. Julie, the sister of the late Céleste Nivelle!' I explained."

V.

The boulevard tide was running strong now. Newsboys, senators, manikins, *chôtneurs*, bards of the cellar cabarets, dowdy English-women with netted hair, sleek clerics — for a minute or two we watched it all in silence.

"I, Lapierre," he resumed, "am hardened to much that is sinister and sad; yet I tell you that what I beheld in the face of Félicien Descartes I would gladly forget. Fear? Rage? Hatred? None of these! But if you can picture a man who has been in hell, and who thinks he has made good his escape from that abode of lost souls, and who, at the last portal, the outer gate, is plucked back and damned to all eternity, you would see in his eyes what I unwillingly beheld in those of Descartes."

"But what did he say?" I asked.

"Say? Nothing at all. He turned his face from us to the wall, with its golden sheen broken by clusters of tulips."

"But afterward?" I persisted.

"Nor afterward. From that moment until his neck went under the blade of the merciful and ingenious Dr. Guillotine, no word, no syllable, ever passed his lips!"

Nearly a Football Team

Stradivarius O'Toole was the only son of a musical mother and a boss section hand.

Richly dowered with imagination and pugnacity, Stradivarius enrolled in the Department of Archeology of the University of Pennsylvania, and devoted himself with singleness of mind to the subject of football.

All this was far back in the Old Testament era of the game — "an eye for an eye, a tooth for a tooth"; better still, a whole set of teeth, provided the referee was not looking.

It was a day of inhuman mass formations and hellish stratagems; in assembling the teams, the players were gathered as were the biblical wedding guests — by scouring the highways and byways.

O'Toole enjoyed his college career to the dregs.

From time to time he dropped in to a lecture on the early customs of the Hittites, or Assyriology, or the origin of Unitarianism, or whatever lecture might coincide with a leisure hour snatched from training table or field practice; his summers were spent in camp with next year's candidates; he joined an exclusive fraternity, and until snow flew each autumn indulged in a Berserker dream of carnage.

He was a good player in a period when, if a football man after a game found that nothing was broken, he was secretly ashamed, and prone to earnest self-examination lest he might have shirked his duty in some way.

His imagination found nourishment in the constant occurrence of the unexpected. No one knew what the other team might spring in any given game. It might be a layout of patent leather togs well greased, or brass headpieces with spikes in them.

You never could tell; a good coach had to have more imagination than David Belasco; and the rules were elastic enough to suit all temperaments.

After six or seven years on the varsity Stradivarius O'Toole duly accepted an attractive offer to build up a football spirit at the University of Tooloolah. He had a degree (he had transferred to the veterinary department) and a diploma he couldn't read.

Moreover, he had his fill of actual playing, and the offer of five thousand dollars a season and expenses from the president of Tooloolah, a fine old man who wished to increase his enrolment, came at a time when his funds were running low.

He felt at the time that he might have secured more, but he had a fancy to see what he could do in a place where they had never even seen a football and thought a gridiron was something to broil ham on.

Nor did he ever have cause to regret that he had not been swayed by low, mercenary motives, for they used him very white indeed, right out in little old Tooloolah, with a campus a mile square and no city within two hundred miles.

O'Toole was given *carte blanche* for expenses; and, after looking over the three hundred odd cow-punchers and grain-producers in the plant, he saw at once that he had the material for a good, stiff line; but he needed a proper set of backs.

So, after teaching them how to fall on the new balls he imported from home, and how to tackle, he took a flier through Denver, Seattle, and the Frisco docks, looking for worthy young men desirous of enjoying the advantages of culture — physical and otherwise.

He picked up a likely candidate for fullback on Telegraph Hill, San Francisco.

He was asleep when O'Toole found him. After feeling him over he shipped him on to Tooloolah, f. o. b.; and when he woke up he was enrolled in the divinity school. At first he was bewildered, and then he wanted to fight; but the two guards took him out and showed him a few things about varsity life, and he had no money to get back to Frisco with, and did not dare, to go, anyhow, because the police wanted him for a strong-arm job there; so he decided to stick along.

The other three backs O'Toole found in a bunch in a Denver music hall; they were getting seventy-five per for a knockabout act; and when he showed them how easy it was to get twice that and a college education thrown in, to say nothing of trifles like room and board, they never let him out of their sight for a minute till the train pulled out for Kickapoo, which is the junction for Tooloolah.

The line averaged 260 pounds from tackle to tackle, and there wasn't a fat man in it.

The ends were small; in fact, the lightest man only tipped 192; but they could both do better than ten flat for the hundred, and they were all knees and elbows. When they lined up the men were so wide they overlapped their opponents by from six to eight yards, which was a great advantage.

The backs were clever men, but there wasn't a sprinter among them.

At first O'Toole regretted that he had taken them on, because there were men right in Tooloolah who could run rings about them; but he had made contracts with every one, and if he had not used them there would have been an awful yell from the faculty, which was scared already because he had spent so much without a cent of return.

So he decided to adapt his game to their peculiar talents, and let it go at that.

O'Toole made his line so stiff that a rat could not have squeezed through, nor a steamroller gone over it.

It was so stiff that the quarterback sometimes used to change his mind and try a different play after the ball was snapped, and get his backs bunched together and talk it over, and that line would hold all the time till the backs got good and ready to start.

The first game was with Big Horn, which had won all its matches but two the previous season, and which refused to take on Tooloolah until O'Toole placed one hundred bucks where they would do the most good, and also let it leak out that his men were backing their team.

That settled it; and when they lit out for Big Horn, out of a total registration of 310, they carried 308; and one man was in the infirmary with measles. The fellows brought all the money they could beg, borrow, or steal; and some of them who had no real money brought chickens, white mice, overcoats, and watches; and one chap took the set of Daniel Webster's speeches from the college library.

If they had lost, half the college would have had to go to jail, and all of them would have had to walk home. For real sporting blood, the East has little on the West!

Before the game O'Toole took the umpire and referee aside and told them it had got to be a square deal or a free fight, and in the latter case most any one was liable to get accidentally disabled. They were nice young men from a freshwater college, and very reasonable.

Big Horn won the toss, and in just three plays put the ball over and kicked a goal.

Their halves were half-breeds, and no one could get anywhere near them — not even their own interference. The noise was awful — except where Tooloolah sat. Then sides were changed.

Ruell, the Tooloolah fullback, went outside of tackle for ten yards. He was six feet ten inches tall, all bone and sinew, and he ran so low he looked like a dachshund.

He got five more in the same place, and then Big Horn's line held. Then O'Toole called back his guards, who weighed 570 between them, and they made holes in Big Horn's line which looked like volcanic craters; and finally Ruell went over for a touchdown, followed by a goal.

Each side got another touchdown before time was called, and in the intermission the two sides of the field used such language to each other that more than two hundred reasonable, hardened spectators left the field.

On the line-up, O'Toole tried out a new formation he had invented.

The team formed a wedge, with their arms about each other's waists and their heads down. Only, instead of starting back twenty yards or so, he started them clear back of their own goal posts, and by the time they reached mid-field they were going so fast they looked like a blur on the landscape.

Just as they reached the line the quarter put the ball in play, passed it to an end, and fell in behind; and when they struck Big Horn it was like a six-cylinder touring-car going through a mud puddle at sixty-five miles an hour. The opposing players were tossed up in the air for ten feet.

Tooloolah went clear to their five-yard line, and would have gone over if the man carrying the ball had not turned his ankle. On the next play a fumble gave Big Horn the ball.

She could not use her speedy halves, for O'Toole had drawn both ends well out on one side of the line, and both halves on the other, and each pair laid for one of Big Horn's halves; and when they tackled they put their elbows into them wherever there was a soft spot and fell on them.

Both men went out within five minutes of the beginning of the second half, and the substitutes were nowhere nearly so good.

By this time Big Horn was pretty well used up, and began putting in substitutes.

The nineteenth sub was a puny chap who lasted long enough to make just one play, but that play was a goal from the field. That put his team in the lead, and there were left only ten minutes to play.

O'Toole saw he must produce the best he had, or it was all up with Tooloolah; so he was obliged to show his hand, which he had hoped not to have to do till the game with Arizona. So he signaled his quarter to start the falling-tower formation.

In this play the three Guglielmos, whom he had fished out of Denver, lined up as follows: one of the halves mounted the other's shoulders and the little quarter mounted his, with one of the ends drawn back to act as quarter in his place.

When the ball was snapped he threw it up to the quarter, and the three men then toppled slowly over like they did in one of their music-hall acts; and, of course, they fell forward not less than five or six yards, and the quarter jumped forward two or three more just as he landed.

The line charged forward and prevented Big Horn from bearing him back; it was first down every time.

Big Horn was simply crazy.

She tried to break the Tooloolah line and get at the leaning tower before it commenced to lean; but Tooloolah had a line that year that did not know how to yield an inch. Then they tried to get the quarter as soon as he dropped within reach, and beat him back; but he came down like a catapult, with his hobnailed boots spread out feeling for their heads, and he wore a pneumatic suit O'Toole had specially designed for him, so he was not a bit fussy how he fell.

Then they tried forming an opposition tower, but they were not used to it, and fell all over themselves, and this completed their demoralization.

They were so rattled that at their fifteen-yard line O'Toole formed a fake tower and then sent Ruell around their end for a touchdown, and they were so excited trying to get at the human tower they never even saw Ruell, and no one tried to stop him.

Tooloolah took back one thousand five hundred dollars in gate money, and within three weeks her enrolment had increased to over five hundred.

Chancellor Egghedd, of Tooloolah, was one of the most lovable of men. After the victory over Big Horn he called Stradivarius O'Toole into his office one night to congratulate him on his work.

"Mr. O'Toole," said he, "you have done more for the cause of higher education in Tooloolah than any man on our faculty. You are the Friedrich Froebel of the plains."

"Yes, sir," said O'Toole, fishing in the dusty archives of his memory for some hint as to who this man Froebel was, and where he had played. "I did my best, sir."

"I have, as you know," continued Chancellor Egghedd, "a great abhorrence for gambling. It has ruined more promising young lives than any other single vice. 'Wine, gambling, and close harmony,' as the German poet, freely translated, has said, are the bane of undergraduate life. Have you any reason to suspect that any of my young men have indulged in mercenary speculation upon the outcome of the late football match?"

"Well, chancellor," replied O'Toole, "the local liverymen and tobacconists have worn an air of unwholesome cheerfulness since the game, and prosperity has laid its chill hand on the sacred purlieus of the campus. Being of a deeply suspicious nature, I had feared that certain careless students might have profited by the last touchdown we made!"

The chancellor sighed.

"I must look into it," he declared. "I have given to Tooloolah the best ten years of my life, and last year my salary was raised to one thousand eight hundred dollars. By strictest economy I have saved up five hundred dollars against my old age, and I am going to ask you, Mr. O'Toole, a great favor; nothing less than to take this little nest-egg and invest it for me where it will do the most good.

"A man in your position must see many opportunities for increasing a modest stake. I shall not ask any details; only, of course, do not forget that I abhor betting in any form."

O'Toole wrung the chancellor's hand until he winced, and as a wringer he was peerless. Then he took his five hundred dollars and faded out into the night. He was very fond of Chancellor Egghedd, who was an extremely nervous man, with one glass eye.

In conversation, when he warmed up to his subject, he would absentmindedly remove this eye and polish it vigorously with a red silk handkerchief, holding it up to the light from time to time to scrutinize it, and when he replaced it it signified that the interview was at an end.

O'Toole's mind was now bent on winning the next game which was against Arizona.

The victory against Big Horn was needed, as it gave the team and the college confidence in his methods and their own abilities; but Big Horn had never even scored on Arizona, which was a classy football college, some of whose players occasionally got into the all-America selection.

How to defeat them with his willing but inexperienced team O'Toole did not know.

He had relied on his falling-tower formation for at least one touchdown, but had been obliged to use that to pull out the Big Horn game, and of course Arizona would devise a successful defense for it, now that it was public property, for the daily press was full of it.

Unless, however, Tooloolah could defeat Arizona, there was little chance of bringing about the Eastern tour, which was so essential to O'Toole's proposed campaign. He therefore called a mass-meeting of students one night and addressed them as follows:

"Fellows: If Tooloolah will do exactly as I say for three weeks every man jack of you can get his hooks on as pretty a piece of money as he will ever see at one time. The odds against us are now five to one, and they are going to be much longer.

"It is up to you to hock everything you own and back the team for the limit, for if we win we can never again get any such odds, and if we lose we don't lose very much, as we have the short end. I am going to put up all I own, and Chancellor Egghedd — er — that is," said O'Toole, recollecting himself, "must, of course, know nothing about it, as he abhors gambling.

"I want every man who weighs over ninety-six pounds to report tomorrow for practice. Not one of you know his possibilities. I do, once I see you in action. I am going to comb Tooloolah with a fine-tooth comb, and I want at least six elevens on the field every blessed afternoon from 1 p.m. till candlelight."

The applause was deafening, and next day O'Toole had so many candidates that he had to work them in shifts, and the third and fourth teams played from midnight to dawn and slept daytimes.

O'Toole was a stickler for discipline, and tolerated no levity on the gridiron. "Merry quips are well enough for the classroom, fellows," he told them, "and a little romping is not inapropos in faculty meetings, but remember, out here we are engaged in serious work, and your horny-handed fathers did not send you to college to fritter away your time, and your sainted mothers would exude bitter, bitter tears were they to know that their cherished ones were wasting the brightest years of their young lives."

Half the subs and some of the regulars were sniveling by this time, and even O'Toole himself was affected. After that he had no trouble from lack of seriousness.

The day shift, comprising some eighty men, rose at seven, took a cross-country run, and ate a light breakfast of eggs, cereals, tea, toast, English bloaters, chicken livers, and bacon.

They then assembled in the chapel, where O'Toole outlined to them the day's work, pointing out the errors of the preceding day. At ten o'clock the entire squad practiced falling on the ball, passing, drop-kicking, and tackling for an hour, after which they attended lectures and recitations till half past eleven.

Then dinner was served, consisting of rare beef, celery, custards, cold slaw, and a bottle of stout each. After dinner came a nap of an hour, and then the real work began on the gridiron and lasted till about five o'clock, when the men were rubbed down and given a simple supper of prunes, guava jelly, toast, tea, and cold meat.

In the evening O'Toole gave an hour's talk in the chemical laboratory, which had been turned over to his use, illustrating on the big blackboards various formations and their proper defense, and trying to impress upon them the necessity of every man being in every play and doing something if it were nothing more than trying to spike his opponent.

Immediately after the lecture the squad was put to bed.

When you pause to consider that in addition to this O'Toole had to coach the night shift from midnight till dawn, give them also a short talk during their supper, which took place at 6 a.m. sharp, and attend to his press work besides, it will be understood that he was far from being an idle, dissipated man.

Incidentally, all the faculty, the janitor, the cooks and waiters had entrusted him with various sums, totaling about thirteen thousand dollars, which he felt it his duty to place as advantageously as possible, realizing that, were he to lose it, Tooloolah would be no place for him.

The isolation of the college was very advantageous to his press campaign.

No stranger could come to town without being spotted at once; it was too remote for sporting reporters to visit, and the real state of affairs could be shrouded in a mystery impossible for a city institution to maintain. O'Toole saw to it that the worst possible rumors percolated into the sporting columns of the dailies.

Anarchy reigned at Tooloolah; the faculty was seriously inclined to abolish football altogether. Ruell had water on the brain, and it was doubtful if he played again this season; one of our guards had broken both ankles; our captain had resigned in a fit of the grouch, and an unpopular man had been chosen to succeed him.

Tooloolah had no back who could kick a ball straight for thirty yards; all the quarters mixed their signals and demoralized the team; the third eleven had held the varsity for no score, and so on, items familiar to every follower of the sporting columns during October and early November.

Under O'Toole's skilful manipulation the odds against Tooloolah rose not only to fifteen to one, but five to one was offered that Arizona would not be scored on. O'Toole then played his trump card. There was at Tooloolah a strapping young Hoosier named Hosea Higgins.

He weighed about two hundred and fifty, and his chest was as round as a barrel, and a great scar on his face where he had enjoyed an attack of ringworm in early youth gave him an expression of exceeding brutality. But Higgins was as soft as blancmange, and had such a serious heart lesion that he could not even hurry to catch a train.

O'Toole took him aside and explained just what he was to do, and packed him off to Arizona, where presently he spread frightful rumors of the state of affairs at Tooloolah, where he had been playing a phenomenal game at tackle, he told them, but had resigned in disgust because the entire team was going to the bow-wows, it being impossible to get the men out to practice, half of them being drunk every night and the other half with heavy conditions to work off in the classroom.

The effect was instantaneous; odds rose to twenty to one on Arizona.

They tried hard to get Hosea on their team, but he declared that loyalty forbade him to line up against his dear old playmates, nor would he divulge their signal code. This caused his reports to be implicitly believed.

Tooloolah now began to place her money in small blocks, and as inconspicuously as possible; however, the thousands covered, caused the odds to sag a little; but every one got in at not worse than fifteen to one, and Tooloolah stood in to take more money out of Arizona than their entire college plant was worth, provided she won.

Examinations were entirely abolished by a unanimous faculty vote for the remainder of the football season.

Never had O'Toole met such hearty cooperation or a more liberal body of educators. They talked of trips to Europe, a new library, and other things — though not one of them ever hinted where they expected to get the money from.

Meanwhile, O'Toole was worried blue over his offense. The line grew better and better. He took them out on the prairie one day when the curious, dingy, yellow sky promised a cyclone, and when the great funnel-shaped hurricane hit them not a man budged from his place.

It was a fool trick, though, for a grand piano, carried along by the wind from an adjoining State, caught one of the tackles on the side of the head, and he was out of the game for three precious days.

The three Guglielmos had nothing to take the place of their falling tower formation; and Ruell, while a good ground gainer, could not kick over seventy yards, and seldom made more than twenty at a time through the line.

Just as O'Toole was at his wits end Baba Maratta came to Tooloolah to study western theology.

He was a high-caste Hindu, a real one, with a turban and flowing robes, and he was so fussy he would eat nothing except what he cooked himself — and he was one of the worst cooks in the world. One morning, as O'Toole was returning from coaching the night squad, he came upon Baba Maratta on the campus, whirling about like an enormous top, his robes standing out like those of Loie Fuller and his eyes glaring like search-lights.

O'Toole thought he had gone crazy, and hung round to see how matters fell out; but presently the Baba stopped and explained that this was a religious rite, and that his people were whirling dervishes, and had been that way since before the flood.

So, while the student body was at chapel (all except those who were excused because of football), he thought it a good time to go through his own devotions for the day.

O'Toole thought no more of it at the time, but that night after lecture it suddenly popped into his fertile mind what an awfully hard man he would be to tackle. To be sure, he was making no forward progress; but could he not? Not a wink did he sleep till he had seen him and unburdened his mind.

At first he was inclined to feel insulted; but O'Toole pointed out to him that he might be able to introduce the peculiar virtues of his sect to great multitudes of people who otherwise would die in sinful ignorance, and he fell for it and agreed to come out for the night shift.

He stampeded the fourth team at once, as they thought him a ghost; but when they understood matters they were mightily interested.

O'Toole soon found that Baba could move in any direction at will while continuing to spin. One of the instructors in mathematics discovered that he revolved at an average speed of three hundred and six times a minute. He was started zigzagging through the scrubs, and no one could stop him.

It is nearly impossible to tackle a live man revolving three hundred times a minute; the tacklers were thrown off by centrifugal energy. Nor was it easy to trip him up, for his motion was that of a gyroscope, and hence self-steadying, so that wherever he stumbled or was pushed he continued to spin along, maintaining his equilibrium.

After a few nights' practice Baba mastered the signals, and that was all O'Toole wished him to do, as he did not propose to use him in any mass plays and take chances on a broken leg.

He brought him out against the varsity, and he sifted through them as lightly as a bit of thistledown. Once in a while some one would get a clutch that brought him down, but O'Toole obviated this by having a special suit made for him of stiff, shiny patent-leather, well padded.

After that he went where he pleased. He seemed to enjoy himself, as he explained that it all counted for piety, and would give him a great boost in his next incarnation.

No man who was present will ever forget the day of the Arizona game. Just how many spectators were present will never be known. There were over thirty thousand tickets sold besides the passes, and in addition an enterprising house in Tucson flooded the country with counterfeits, the holders of which, being desperate men, insisted on squeezing in, and that must have added ten thousand more.

Then there were several hordes of cowpunchers, miners, and rustlers who stormed the gates and got in without any tickets at all

Walter Camp came all the way from New Haven in a special, and all the great dailies sent experts, while in the press-box sat the Duc d'Abruzzi, Elbert Hubbard, and Gunboat Smith.

The grand stands swayed and creaked like laboring, ships, and the din was so terrific that experts in the city of Mexico announced well-defined seismographic disturbances.

At precisely two-thirty Tooloolah trotted out on the field one hundred and ten men, headed by the giant Ruell, bearing the pale-green banner of the college — with its seal and historic motto — "*Vincite aut Eviscite*" (win or eviscerate) ; every man determined to live up to it this day.

Arizona followed with a squad of equal size. After a brief period of warming up Tooloolah won the toss, and at once started her famous wedge 'way back under the south grand stand.

It was beautifully executed, and struck Arizona in one solid mass, traveling a shade better than ten seconds flat; yet, incredible as it may seem, it not only failed to make an inch, but was actually thrown back for a couple of yards. The Arizona line was not as heavy, but it was all sinew and gristle. They lined up with four miners, three Mexican matadors, two Nez Percé Indians, a well-known pugilist, and one other player O'Toole had been unable to get a line on. They were all students in good standing and members of the best frats in Arizona.

On second down Tooloolah at once tried the falling tower, with the three Guglielmos mounted on one another's shoulders, and little Bill tumbled forward for seven yards, making it first down.

Twice more they made their distance, and then Arizona met it with a successful counter tower, which toppled into it and crumpled it up for no gain.

Then Ruell was sent between guard and center for fifteen yards, and again just inside of tackle for ten, more, andthen Arizona held tight and Tooloolah had to kick.

Arizona could do nothing on the offense; Tooloolah's line that year could not be pierced by any engine, human or mechanical. Once in a while one of the Nez Percé Indians skirted their opponents' ends for a good gain, and three times their fullback just missed kicking a field goal; but the half ended scoreless.

During the intermission three men were shot and one stabbed, and there was a lynching; but the noise was so tremendous few knew about it at the time save the parties directly concerned.

Right in the center of the west stand sat Chancellor Egghedd, the gleam of sunlight on his glass eye as he polished it feverishly, while he fixed the empty socket upon O'Toole in mute but agonizing appeal.

There is no need to rehearse the details of this game, which have been ably analyzed by Mr. Camp in the three-volume history he devotes to it.

Every football lover knows how the game see-sawed back and forth, and how the spectators were now raised to delirious joy, now sunk in hideous despair. With only ten minutes left to play, O'Toole put in Baba Maratta, who waltzed out in his shiny black suit amid a hush of expectancy.

Arizona at once protested and drew the color line. O'Toole had to prove to them that Baba was a genuine Hindu, of a family whose antiquity made King Solomon look like a vulgar upstart.

When the matter was adjusted and the teams lined up it was found that the timekeeper had been so absorbed in the dispute that he had forgotten to take time out, and only four minutes were left.

Two or three more were wasted by scrapping in the line, and when at last the ball was passed to Baba it was a question whether he could make his run and beat put the whistle.

He stood so far back that Arizona expected a kick, and spread out for one. When he began slowly to revolve she was stumped, and had no idea what was up. The spectators were so stupefied that not a sound came from the stands.

Faster and faster Baba revolved (it always took him some time to get steam up, and his team had been drilled to protect him during this chrysalis state). Two or three Arizonians skirted the ends and bore down on him, only to be blocked by our backs, when suddenly, just as their quarter dove for him, he shot off on a tangent and was away.

Never was seen the like of that run.

His own team scattered; there was; more danger of their obstructing Baba than helping him. What he needed was room. Up and down he spun, always whirling like a black diamond in the sun.

The Arizona tacklers who touched him glanced off like skipping stones, while nearer and nearer their goal twisted Baba Maratta in an intricate and pleasing spiral. He was as hard to hold as a drop of quicksilver on a hot stove, and he had threaded the entire team of frantic Arizonians, who were bumping into each other and falling all over themselves in their eagerness, when O'Toole saw the timekeeper put the whistle to his lips — and Baba still five yards away!

One of the inspirations which come to men of genius seized upon him. Stooping and seizing a small rock, he hurled it and knocked the whistle ten yards away, and Baba slanted over the line and Tooloolah had won the game.

The goal was never kicked, for reasons connected with the audience. Besides, Tooloolah didn't need it.

Overcome by emotion, for the first and only time in his life O'Toole fainted away. When he recovered he was in his room at Tooloolah, and the whole place was littered up with the gold and greenbacks which represented his share of the winnings.

Not a menial employee around the place cleaned up less than a thousand dollars, and good old Chancellor Egghedd went on a three days' bat, although he had been a strict teetotaler for over twenty years.

For three years in all Stradivarius O'Toole remained at Tooloolah, and in that time the college increased from a bare three hundred to over fifteen hundred. At the same time the city of Kickapoo increased from eight hundred to five thousand; and seven churches, a bank, nine gents' furnishing stores, over twenty first-class saloons, two undertaking establishments, four liveries, and a few hotels owe to him their existence.

During his entire career he kept steadily in view his great and climacteric exploit, "the invasion of the East." To this end he bent every resource of a really remarkable and versatile mind.

His team cleaned up everything within two hundred miles, and the local museum contains over one hundred costly trophies won during those five memorable years. The college groaned under bequests, and the gymnasium, fraternity houses, and campus were the wonder of the West.

At length the time came when he felt that his warriors were trained to the minute and that his skill could carry them no further.

Like Napoleon, he personally oversaw every detail of the proposed campaign; human foresight could do no more. The memorable October arrived when the Tooloolah all-star aggregation pulled out of Kickapoo Junctions for its long Eastern tour. They traveled in three sections.

The first consisted of six baggage-cars and a perambulating gymnasium and shower-bath combination. The second consisted of a dining car, smoker, and four coaches, and carried six surgeons, ten osteopaths, ten trained nurses, a veterinary, two general practitioners, a pharmacist, manicure, four barbers, and twenty rubbers.

The third section carried the team itself; sixty-five members in all, and consisted of a dining car, combination barbershop, observation and library car, and five Pullmans.

Progress was one continued ovation. Every town met them with delegations of leading citizens and long lines of little schoolgirls in white, bearing huge nosegays of sweet-Williams, marigolds, petunias, and bachelor-buttons. Speeches were made by selectmen, postmasters, mayors, and village orators. Census reports show that over two hundred babies were christened "Stradivarius" during the period of the tour.

It is no exaggeration to say that, had O'Toole so desired, he could have been elected to any office for which he was eligible in the West, and his features on banners, triumphal arches, and billboards were better known than those of the late Mrs. Pinkham or the genial Mr. Mennen.

O'Toole, however, fixed his eye singly upon one goal alone — the subjugation of the effete East.

Who could have foreseen disaster as his magnificent cortege swept toward the Atlantic, accompanied by paeans of applause? But, like Napoleon, his cohorts were destined to perish miserably amid the snows of an inhospitable clime. He, too, was to behold his Moscow.

Never was a football team so wonderfully equipped with knowledge of the game, proper paraphernalia, and able exponents.

Here was good old Ruell, reliable as ever. There were the three Guglielmos, now sophomores. There was the Whirling Dervish, elusive as of old. And there were a host of new men; Professor Jonas Verbena (to name but two) and Hoganowski, the Russian dog-faced boy, the latter with a car all to himself and a nice pile of sand in which to bury his bones and dog biscuit.

Baba Maratta had half a car, also, with a complete kitchenette and an imported Hindu cook belonging to his own caste. Nothing had been left undone, and the corporation of Tooloolah University had spared no expanse, realizing that the invasion was the biggest advertisement their college could possibly get, as every mile was reported in the press and leading magazines.

A record-smashing crowd gathered at Cornell to witness the first game. Owing to a broken rail, the train pulled late into Ithaca, and the Cornell team had already run through their signal, drill when Tooloolah appeared before the expectant throng.

Perfect silence prevailed as the army of football warriors swung through the south gate, headed by Ruell bearing the pale-green banner with its grim legend Rank after rank followed him in a silence so profound that the scraping of their spiked shoes could be heard throughout the giant coliseum. When directly opposite the press-box the squad lined up and hurled forth their defiant battle-cry:

> *We are the men from the woolly West;*
> *Death to us is a merry jest!*
> *Ours is the team that never fails,*
> *Our only food is rusty nails;*
> *Human gore is our only drink,*
> *And we're kind and gentle, we don't think!*
> *Tooloolah!*

Immediately after ranks broke and the team trotted out, ready to begin the conquest of the East.

Cornell won the toss, and, having felt out our line a couple of times, punted to little Guglielmo, who fumbled. A Cornell end gathered in the ball and ran the length of the field for a touchdown. The truth is O'Toole's men were a bit rusty after their long journey, and this reverse was exactly what they needed to rouse their fighting spirit.

Relying strictly on straight football they scored three touchdowns during the remainder of the half, leaving the score eighteen-six in their favor.

In the second half O'Toole replaced the old veteran Ruell by one of his freaks, Clarence Meringue, whose fame had not penetrated east of the Mississippi at that time.

Clarence was one of the most graceful pole-vaulters ever seen. Using a ten-foot pole and carrying the ball in his teeth, clenched firmly to the lacing, he started about twenty yards back of the line, whose flanks were strengthened by the two halves drawn out for that purpose.

Running easily forward and striking his pole about two yards back of center, he rose like a bird in the air, and at the apex of his flight flung himself forward over the heads of the opposing line and even at times beyond their secondary defense. Wearing a pneumatic suit, he dropped from the sky into the midst of the disgusted Cornelians, clearing from five to seven yards at a time. No defense was adequate against this play, provided his line held; and it did. That was what it was there for!

O'Toole's theories were once more justified; and the size of the score was merely limited to the time it took Clarence Meringue to hop up and down the length of the field. In this case he made eight touchdowns. In this game the low, professional tone of Eastern college morals became evident:

Although nothing could be found in the rules which referred to the use of a pole-vaulted in football, O'Toole having merely been the only coach imaginative enough to use one, Pennsylvania, his next opponent, notified him that the game would be canceled unless he agreed to extinguish Clarence Meringue. From a reliable source it was learned that Mr. Walter Camp was directly responsible for this low subterfuge.

Rather than forego the pleasure of walloping Penn, O'Toole signaled "23" to Clarence and sent him weeping to his tent.

Determined to have revenge on his old alma mater, O'Toole decided to use Hoganowski, the Russian dog-faced boy, whom he has intended to reserve for Yale. Material was so plentiful that he believed himself justified, not apprehending the series of unparalleled disasters which were in store.

Ruell's phenomenal ability to run low has been spoken of. Well, Hoganowski ran lower. In fact, he ran on all fours, and was a terror at gaining ground after being tackled.

He was a good, willing fellow, not brilliant mentally (he had never been able to learn to read or write, and was enrolled in the anthropological department), but was endowed with grand football instinct. Like Clarence, he carried the ball in his teeth, and would make anywhere from three to ten yards with half a dozen tacklers on top of him, growling and frothing and shaking his shaggy head.

He made eleven touchdowns that day, but they did him up at last, poor chap.

He was buried next day. The floral tributes were beautiful. The team sent a vast collar of violets, with the word "Fido" picked out in white immortelles. One of the men, a fine student, selected the word because he said it was Latin for "faithful."

From Pennsylvania the team went directly to Princeton, where O'Toole electrified the Tigers by introducing the Bras de Per brothers. Their specialty was to seize little Bill Guglielmo, who received the ball on a double pass, swing him by the legs and arms and hurl him bodily over the opposing rush-line for, many yards.

Bill was an adept in the use of his elbows and knees, and gouged out nine Princeton eyes that glorious afternoon as he was being tackled in the air. No use talking, those orange-and-black chaps are gritty!

O'Toole varied the play by using the three Guglielmos as a human staircase, up whose backs Ruell ran at full speed carrying the ball, and leaping boldly into space over the two struggling lines. When these two plays had drawn the whole Princeton team into a bunch Ruell was sent round the ends on fake formations.

The score was fifty-six to nothing.

When Tooloolah reached Cambridge they had the Crimsons at sea. They had been frantically coaching on all sorts of freak plays, trying to devise some sort of defense for O'Toole's marvelous attacks.

They were tremendously in earnest, and had really worked up a pretty decent sort of a defense to two or three of the formations. Seeing how matters lay, O'Toole changed his tactics entirely and played, a simple rushing game with no tricks whatever.

This caught Harvard entirely unprepared, and she was simply overwhelmed. Thus O'Toole followed the rule of the great Napoleon and struck the enemy where he did not expect the blow. Besides, he thus reserved his remaining stratagems for Yale, whom he met in the final and culminating game.

The game was to be the apotheosis of his career; the end he had kept in mind for five long years. Well he knew that New Haven was in a state of nervous tension impossible to describe. He had seen her scouts in increasing numbers shivering on the sidelines of the bloody field of his inexorable progress.

Mr. Walter Camp had been kept up only by the copious use of bromides, alternated with hypodermic injections of strychnine, in order that he might devote every moment to the team. And a superb eleven had been the result — the best Eli ever turned out.

This was just what O'Toole desired, and when he swung aboard his Pullman at Boston after seeing his team safely aboard he fully expected to see the sun rise in New Haven on an O'Toole Austerlitz. But alas for the careful plans of a mere man!

Hoganowski was lost and Clarence Meringue barred from further competition.

Ruell, the iron man, had at last broken an instep, and two of the Guglielmo trio had splintered kneecaps. The line, also, while intact, was very fine and lean as so many rats.

But these were merely the chances of war — chances O'Toole had allowed for — the final catastrophe was yet to come. Between Springfield and Hartford the first section was derailed and the following section crashed into it, and by a horrible irony of fate every blessed remaining one of the peerless aggregation of backs was either killed outright or maimed beyond hope of recovery.

The most grievous loss was that of Professor Jonas Verbena, who had been kept so carefully under cover that even O'Toole's own team had no idea what part he was destined to play. He had discovered Professor Verbena at the time when he was taking a P. G. course in experimental psychology at Tooloolah and had used him in but one game.

He was a thin, hairy, feeble old man, and even in the specially padded suit he wore his frailty was only too evident. Hypnotism was his specialty; and in the game with Peoria he had hypnotized their entire team, so that when Ruell received the ball Peoria gathered in a little bunch in the middle of the field and began to sing that heartrending ballad, "There stood my poor old father, weeping at the bar!"

Meanwhile, Ruell centered down the field for a touchdown, with no one even trying to stop him.

Of course, no one knew what had happened but Professor Verbena and O'Toole; the audience, which had backed Peoria at ruinous odds, thought they had been sold out by their team and chased them off the field and well into the adjoining State; and the game went to Tooloolah, five to nothing.

The affair was a great mystery, and as much so to Tooloolah as to everybody else. From that day O'Toole had saved up Professor Verbena for the Yale game.

As to that game, suffice it to say that Tooloolah was compelled to go up against Mr. Camp's team with a very much shaken line and a set of backs not one of whom had O'Toole dreamed of using, and none of whom was phenomenal.

In vain his gallant line held like a rock against the charges of Yale; in vain the crippled Ruell plowed into that husky hunch of blue. As a last resort, O'Toole had fitted out his team with pneumatic suits, so that when Yale charged they would rebound from them.

The score was a tie. In O'Toole's supreme battle he had failed to win; and fond hope of years was dashed to earth

Tooloolah would even have been scored upon by a phenomenal Yale placement kicker had O'Toole not invented a defense akin to his human tower, which lined up in front of the goal-posts, so that little Bill Guglielmo could jump and block the ball. This was the only bright spot in the game.

Rendered bitter by his ill fortune, O'Toole abdicated. Learning that a coed school in New Mexico was in need of an instructor in prisoner's base, he applied for the position and passed into voluntary retirement and obscurity.

Thus went Napoleon to St. Helena.

Desperate Remedies

Ezra Ransom sat in the Louis Quatorze dining room of his double suite in the Hysteria Apartment House, unhappily breakfasting.

He liked neither the room, the service, nor the breakfast. He was willing to concede that the Louises of France were not without renown as kings, but as interior decorators he regarded them as distinctly punk. He wished that any of them might have seen how a modern white enamel and glass dairy lunch is equipped.

He would greatly have preferred to be down in Callahan's, where the waiter chatted with him about the latest sayings of his little boy, and discussed the local political situation with refreshing idiom and a homely shrewdness.

As for Willing, the man who was waiting upon him in his own home, Ransom did not even know whether or not he were married, and dared not ask. The second Mrs. Ransom tolerated no familiarity with or from her servants; and he was too kindhearted to imperil Willing's job. The latter had a habit of appearing noiselessly at the master's side, with a whispered query from lips that never seemed to move and a face that belonged distinctly to high-grade poker.

He appeared now, serving ham and eggs. Ransom noted disgustedly that the oval silver platter bore a garnishing border of parsley: a botanical specimen he considered fit neither to eat nor wear, and hence, as an efficiency expert, felt to be senseless waste. The eggs, too, were "sunny-side up," an error Callahan would never have made.

The ceremony of pouring coffee, with its two lumps, the thick cream, then the amber fluid added slowly and simultaneously with hot milk, seemed to him as tedious as a Japanese tea ritual.

The hour was ten—unprecedented in his routine. He was out-raging all his instincts in order to have a paternal chat with Ezra junior, his only child, and a youth difficult to catch after his late breakfast.

The boy, a clean-cut, alert-looking chap of twenty-four, entered as his father finished eating and absent-mindedly tipped the scandalized Willing a quarter.

"Greetings and salutations!" he cried, as he sank into the opposite chair. "Why the late hours?"

Ezra senior, a close observer of men, noted the subtle difference with which Willing hovered about the younger man's chair. It was nothing tangible—one could not say that there was any more respectful or efficient service—but Willing seemed to be thinking "here, at last, I am serving a gentleman!" All this with no change in his expression, save a different light in his eyes, a slight variation in the angle of his bent spine.

The boy chose deviled kidneys, sent them back with a languid flow of abuse, ordered a Spanish omelet in its place, nibbled at it, and Ransom could see that he had gained caste. He wondered vaguely at it. He was paying the running expenses of the establishment, yet had not been able to make any notable impression upon Willing. His son, to whom he gave a liberal allowance, bore with the matchless *savoir-faire* of the second generation, an air of condescending proprietorship.

When he had been served to his liking, the elder drew forth a little paper packet of three mild five-cent cigars, lighted one from the match held by Willing, and answered his son's query.

"This is an unusual hour for me to be breaking my fast, Ezra, and one that it would be hard indeed for me to accustom myself to. My object was to have a little chat with you; and you are a hard bird to snare once you leave the house."

Ezra junior speared a fresh mushroom with his fork, and examined it critically.

"Glad you waited for me," he said easily. "I am a pretty busy cit-izen these days, I'll admit."

The father puffed reflectively before replying.

"I don't know that I should use the word 'busy'; I am sorry to have to say it of my only son, but I should call you a very idle citizen. A non-producer—the first one of your family."

A slightly bored look crossed the boy's face. This was not the first conversation they had held on the subject.

"I know we can never agree on this topic, dad, but I'm honestly convinced that I'm right!"

"There are no two ways about it! You are deadwood in the body politic. You consume, and make no return. You eat and drink and play, and pay nothing for it all. The rest of the world has to work a little harder and go without a little more to make up for what you don't do."

The son dipped his fingers into a bowl of warm, perfumed water, dried them, and lighted a fat monogrammed cigarette from a gold case.

"Do you advertise in the papers for help?" he asked with seeming irrelevance.

"Certainly not; we are never short of help. We have a waiting list of capable and industrious young men anxious to connect themselves with our concern."

"Yet you are always trying to get me, the least capable of young men, to go to work for you. By your own statement, if I were to accept, I'd simply crowd out somebody else, who probably could not afford my leisure and would not know how to employ it half so well!"

"You would certainly not be permitted to crowd anybody out. You would receive a sound training in all the departments, from the bottom of the ladder up, and in time the Ransom blood in you would come to the surface, and you would become an asset to us!"

"You do things pretty well here, dad. Are you living right up to your income?"

"No intelligent man spends his entire income, large or small!"

"And I suppose in the natural course of events I will be your heir?"

"That is so."

"Then, as you spend less than you earn, and it's all accumulating for me, I wouldn't become any more valuable to society by giving up everything I like to do, putting on an alpaca jacket and a green shade, and punching a time-clock. I'd merely be making more money for myself. I'm no miser!"

Ransom senior viciously flicked the ash of his cigar onto a costly Kurdistan rug, and scowled at his bland heir.

"The proposition has nothing to do with the amount of money you inherit from me! It has to do with your intelligent care of it. The floral emblems on my grave will not have to wilt before they will be taking it away from you. I insist upon your having at least sufficient business training to take care of what it has cost me so much toil and thought to acquire. When I was your age—"

"I know, father; when you were my age somebody gave you half a buck for stopping a runaway horse, and so started you in life. And when you felt real devilish, you went out back of the barn and played seven-up for beans, and smoked sweet-fern cigarettes. But if you're really afraid the wise boys will get to me when you have gone, why not leave everything to me in trust? I can worry along on five per cent."

An angry red suffused Ransom's face and as much of his neck as showed above his low collar and string tie. He pounded on the table with force enough to spill his water glass, and the pained face of Willing appeared framed in the doorway of the butler's pantry.

"Ezra, when I feel obliged to leave my property in trust, I'll give it away first! There never has been a Ransom who couldn't manage his own affairs, and if you are going to prove the exception, I'll see that you have no affairs to manage! I mean it, by George!"

The son shrugged languidly.

"I'm grateful, of course, that you are not dissipated," the old gentleman continued. "That would be the last straw. But all you seem to care for is dogs and horses, golf, yachting, house partying, and other utterly frivolous and wasteful pursuits. I'm called a man of my word on the Street, and I tell you in all sincerity, that this is positively the last call. If you do not appear at my office at nine sharp next Monday—I shall be there at eight, but I won't cause too rude a break in your luxurious hours—I shall quietly make a move that I've had in mind for some time.

"It will fall on your head like a thunderbolt, and on the heads of some others as well. It will put you where you'll have to root-hog-or-die. It will fall upon me with equal severity; but I love you enough, and have your welfare so at heart, that I'll stop at no sacrifice to make a man and a Ransom out of you!"

For a long moment the two gazed steady-eyed at one another; then the elder pulled his napkin from his vest, where he always tucked it, and strode from the room.

The younger lighted a fresh cigarette, and touched the call-bell.

"I say, Willing," he remarked to the instantly appearing servitor, "you might fetch me a glass of sherry and bitters!"

The ensuing Monday found Ezra Ransom a bundle of nerves, as he sat in his private office fussily rearranging his desk utensils.

Ezra junior was not in the least nervous. He was, in fact, sound asleep in a room at the Sunnybrook Club after an arduous Sunday pursuing the festive anise-bag with the Sunnybrook pack. No thought of a Monday morning engagement disturbed his healthy and dreamless slumber. He had forgotten all his father had said two hours afterward.

Yet it was destined to prove the most momentous interview of his gladsome young life, had he but known it. He had presumed that his father would cut off his allowance for a time. Such temporary annoyances were always happening in his set—one simply stated the circumstance to his pals, and was tided over till the parental skies cleared. That anything more serious impended did not occur to him.

Promptly at a quarter past nine, Ransom called in Bixby, his private secretary of many years standing. To that stupefied middle-aged automaton, he outlined the unique idea that he had conceived as the sole means of forcing his son to realize the hardpan facts of life.

His idea, briefly stated, embraced the giving away of his entire fortune. This required certain cautious formalities. Ransom was not a rich man, rated by metropolitan standards, but his fortune totaled over a million, and he had made it by hard work, in a day when business opportunities and methods varied widely from those of today.

Of latter years, he had attended numerous directors' meetings, many of them occupying but a few moments with a roll call and a perfunctory vote, followed by a pocketing of the usual gold eagle. He came early to his office and fancied that because he held fifty-one per cent of stock in the Ransom Sales Company, Ltd., he was still an active factor in a business whose details had long since passed into the hands of trained departmental heads.

Were he to give away forthright his holdings, it was conceivable that his wife or son might effect the appointment of a conservator, and any marketable alienist would declare him the victim of senile dementia.

"The idea, Bixby," he said, "is this: My holdings must be converted into cash, or at least into certified checks of some third party, and donated anonymously to the list of charities I have drawn up."

"B—but I don't understand, sir!" protested the puzzled secretary. "You mean that you intend to give away everything you own?"

"For my son's salvation, Bixby! I am only fifty-seven, and my physician has just given me a clean bill of health. I can start all over again and make another fortune before I am really an old man. But as long as I have money my son will continue to be a social parasite. Only when he realizes that he has no prosperous father to fall back on will he get out and hustle for himself.

"Mrs. Ransom, of course, is already taken care of through the prenuptial sum settled upon her in lieu of dower. She cannot maintain our establishment in the Hysteria, but all the furnishings are hers, and she can live in comfort in a less pretentious suite."

"But what will you do, Mr. Ransom?"

"Do? Do, Bixby? With my prestige, my reputation as a financier? Why, I'll simply sit back and decide what opening to accept!"

Bixby coughed deprecatingly.

"Of course, sir, I can see all that. But conditions are not the same as when you got your start!"

"Conditions change, Bixby; but principles remain fixed. The knowledge of human nature, the acumen, industrial facts hold today as they held when I incorporated the Ransom Sales Company. What I did then I can do again."

Bixby maintained a discreet silence.

"In consideration of your long and faithful service, you shall receive from me ten thousand dollars, Bixby. You are to call in all bills due from accounts of my wife and son, and notify the shops that future purchases must be strictly for cash. From the "Blue Book" you will secure a list of my son's clubs, and in like manner liquidate his charges in them. I will advise him that he must resign or continue on his own responsibility.

"As there are bound to be certain outstanding obligations we cannot foresee, I shall place in your hands as trustee the sum of five thousand dollars to cover these, the balance to be paid to me. On this balance I will maintain myself until I accept one or another of the offers which will pour in upon me as soon as it is known that I am available. Thus my son and I will start on equal terms. To him I will give outright one thousand dollars. After that he must paddle his own canoe. It will be the making of my boy, Bixby!"

"He'll probably go to Mrs. Ransom," suggested Bixby.

"Much good it will do him, if he does. He won't get a nickel! Mrs. Ransom, I don't mind telling you, Bixby, regards me as a moneymaking machine, and Ezra as my lucky heir. Directly I have given away my property she won't even bow to either of us if we pass on the street."

The following month was a busy one for the faithful secretary. One by one, and without publicity, the holdings of Ezra Ransom were converted into hard cash, and paid into the hungry coffers of divers charitable organizations. He faded silently from one directorate after another, and ceased to be a factor in the Street. He maintained until the last his office in the Ransom Sales Company, busier than he had been for a generation.

The day came when Ransom ate his last breakfast in the hated Louis Quatorze dining room, facing his son. There was no need of an interview with Mrs. Ransom. He had not spoken to her twice during the past three months, and their financial relations had been settled prior to their marriage. But with Ezra junior, the old gentleman desired a final interview.

He endured the ministrations of the detested Willing until past ten o'clock, when the boy entered languidly and greeted his father with mild surprise.

"Well, my boy," said Ransom after his son had ordered, "I'm afraid you won't see much of me for the present! The truth is, I'm looking for a job."

"Why the camouflage, dad? I'm fearfully dull so early in the morn."

"I said that I was looking for a job! I always try to express my meaning tersely. You may recall that at our last pleasant breakfast together I gave you one final chance to try and make a useful citizen of yourself."

Ezra junior smothered a yawn apologetically.

"Hadn't thought of it since, 'pon honor."

"Also, that if you failed me this time, I should take a very radical step to force you to play the man. I have. I this day completed all details whereby I have disposed of my entire fortune. Mrs. Ransom is, of course, taken care of, although she will hardly be able to maintain this perfectly unnecessary scale of living. But you and I, my son, are practically indigent, and must hunt jobs, or rely upon the charity of our friends, or the usual public organizations."

The boy gazed at his father for the first time with close attention.

"If I didn't know you pretty well," he said at length, "I should say that you had taken to drinking before breakfast."

"You can easily verify all that I have said. I have settled all outstanding bills known to me, including your numerous club dues, so that you can resign from them in good standing. As there are bound to be a few that will crop up later, Bixby is holding a contingent fund to cover such as were incurred prior to today. I am responsible for none thereafter. The balance I shall use during the brief period before I accept a new position."

Ransom drew out a worn leather wallet, and from it took a certified check for one thousand dollars, which he passed across the table.

"As your allowance necessarily ceases now for all time, I am giving you this to tide you over until you find work. Your roadster will easily fetch a good sum if you need more."

"Do you actually expect me to believe you have done this insane thing, dad?" the son asked, as he dazedly folded the check and put it in his pocket. "Beggared yourself, at your age, just to get back at me? Cut off your nose to spite your face?"

"I am fifty-seven years old, and my physician reports my health excellent, thanks to my regular life. Only in this way could I bring home to you how strongly I feel. To save you, I am willing to put myself upon an equal footing—I with the asset of experience, you with that of youth. Your youth I cannot share, but my experience you are always welcome to.

"Had I merely cut off your allowance, you could readily have borrowed of your friends, or of usurers at ruinous interest on your prospects. When the truth is known, as it will soon be, no one will lend you a shilling."

"Well, I have to hand it to you, dad. You're certainly game! But keep away from the parks where the big, gray squirrels live."

Ransom terminated the interview at this point. His wife he did not intend to see at all. Bixby would save him her crocodile tears and reproaches. He had already packed his modest belongings in two big kit bags before coming down to breakfast, and ordered them sent to the Union Club, which address he gave his son. There was nothing among the furnishings or bric-a-brac he cared for, and without the slightest regret he heard the door of his apartment in the Hysteria close behind him for the last time.

He lunched contentedly at Callahan's, chatted with his old waiter about his busy little family, and stupefied him by handing him a hundred dollars in new tens. Later on he attended a photoplay and then wandered over to the Union Club, where he engaged a room.

While winding up his affairs, he had been amazed to learn how numerous were the clubs in which he held membership. He was not at all of the clubman type, and had joined for business reasons, or merely because some friend had asked him to, one after another, until the list rivaled that of his son. Bixby had always audited the bills, made out the checks, and he had signed them automatically.

At once, he resigned from all save the Union, the only one he cared for or frequented. Most of his business cronies belonged, and he liked to lounge in the great leather chairs of its dignified, rather old-fashioned rooms, read the papers, talk, and indulge in an occasional game of whist. He rarely ate there, save at banquets. He preferred Callahan's. As he was a life member with no further dues to pay, it was indubitably the club for him to cleave to.

For a day or two the press featured Ransom's surprising move seriously or frivolously, according to their policies. The underlying reason for his act was known only to Ransom himself, Bixby, and Ezra junior. But the metropolitan reporters guessed with amazing shrewdness the size of the fortune disposed of by rounding up the recent anonymous donations to charity. Ransom secluded himself at the Union Club during this period to avoid reporters.

It particularly irked him that the newspapers were practically unanimous in hinting that his mind was affected. "Eccentric act of elderly capitalist" was one caption that grated on him. All the dailies assumed that he had laid aside a sum ample for his own needs, instancing the fact that he was living at an expensive club. Several hinted broadly that he was taking this course to sever uncongenial domestic bonds. Then the juggernaut of municipal life rolled on, and Ransom was forgotten.

Not in years had he felt such a sense of buoyant freedom. For a long while his life had been far less active than his energy craved. He had created such a perfect machine in the Ransom Sales Company that it practically ran itself. Like most successful men, considerable part of his genius consisted in the ability to pick able heads of departments. Little by little, and unconsciously, he had let go of one string after another, until his office hours, regularly maintained, meant little save an elaborately pigeonholed desk, a stenographer, whose position was a sinecure, a tenuous grasp on the broadened field of operations, and a twiddling of thumbs.

Several times a week he attended directors' meetings and fancied himself still a factor in business circles.

Now, his fortune dissipated—he would have objected strenuously to the word—he prepared with a lively anticipation to resume an active career, and create a new competence by his executive skill. He awaited with confidence the multitudinous demands for his organizing ability.

Somewhat to his chagrin, the demands did not seem to roll in. He sat tranquilly in the Union lounge, and foregathered with his erstwhile associates, played whist, loafed before the sea-coal grate, marked time. One and all greeted him cordially, seemed sincerely glad to see him, congratulated him upon his new freedom; but the conversation seemed to be carefully steered away from the realms of high finance. His old-time friends rambled on about civic conditions, the high cost of living, the war, terrible condition of the streets, Federal control, the discharge of old and valued employees, the necessity for retrenchment; but not one of them approached Ransom with any hint that his experience would be welcomed by them.

Their careful avoidance of all reference to his radical move led him to believe that they agreed with the press that his mentality had become a trifle aberrant.

In time, the uneasy suspicion forced itself upon his perception that if he were to obtain a status in present-day affairs, he must go forth into the highways and byways and seek it. The possibility of having to actually seek employment had never occurred to him. To add to his uneasiness, Bixby called at the Union and rendered him a disturbing balance sheet. A heavy modiste's bill for his wife, and one from his son's expensive English tailor, an appalling invoice from their garage, an interior decorator's charge for remodeling their drawing-room from the period of Louis Quatorze to that of the equally fatuous Louis Quinze, these and similar indebtednesses had cut his contingent fund down to a little less than four hundred dollars, where he had counted upon about three thousand.

The stunning fact, that he, a magnate in a way, was at fifty-seven in possession of but a few paltry dollars, and that no prospective position was in view, did not crush him, because he possessed an iron will and unbounded confidence in his own abilities. It rather dazed him for the moment, and the good Bixby was plainly distressed.

Without daring to come out flat and offer to loan him part or all of his ten thousand-dollar bonus, he repeatedly, in taking leave, emphasized his desire to do "anything" for his old employer that lay within his power. Ransom bowed him out of the club-lounge almost bruskly as he desired to be alone and bring his mind to bear upon the situation. His hand trembled a little as he lighted one of his five-cent cigars; but soon there flared up into the keen, blue eyes behind his spectacles the frosty gleam of battle. The old war-horse rose to the trumpet call.

He was still so convinced that at any moment some one of his friends would approach him with an offer, that he continued for another week to live at the Union, where he was most likely to meet them. He began to throw out hints. "A man rusts out sooner than he wears out!" "Getting bored to death without some regular work to do." And other old saws.

To his lure, his crafty friends replied by advising him to "Let George do it," or urged him to take a trip to Bermuda, or merely laughed as at a capital joke.

It did not occur to Ransom that they lacked courage to offer him any sort of position where his services could be of use to them. The salary such a place would command would be so paltry when compared with Ransom's big income that they feared to insult him.

Then, while they were not so obtuse but they could see he really wished to get into harness again, one and all assumed that he had tucked away a tidy sum. The real situation would have left them as dazed as Ransom himself had been for the moment.

He did not see his son during these days, nor did he care to until he had reestablished himself. Twice he found his card upon returning from luncheon at Callahan's.

At the end of the second week he took a room in an obscure hotel, at a rate of six dollars a week. It was by no means a disreputable house, and was reasonably clean; but he abhorred it from the very first. Never in his life had he stopped in such a place, and in recent years he had patronized the very best, though not the most ostentatious.

He still spent most of his time at the Union, where his mail came. But it was surprising how little mail he received; and the bulk of it was ironically of the begging variety. The odor of money clings long. He had one breezy letter from his son, which he read and reread, and then carefully put away in his worn old wallet. "Dear dad," it ran; "I'll bet you've already made a big start toward another million. Believe me, there was some moaning at the bars when I put out to sea! Where I still am, by the way. But any line sent to me at the Country Club will get me in time. Always aff'y, Ezra, Jr."

He made no effort to get in touch with the boy, however, pending his own uncertainty.

Nights in his little hotel were irksome to him. He slept poorly, and was always conscious of a sort of unwholesome activity going on about him in the dark. Occasionally, in the adjoining chambers, the noise rose to a higher key, as when an all-night poker game wound up with a typical drawn wrangle, or other and more sinister sounds penetrated the flimsy walls. In the dim hall he met furtive figures, sketchily clad, scurrying to and from the bathroom.

For these reasons, as well as the steady diminishing of his little hoard, he moved once more, this time to a three-dollar room in a dingy lodging-house in the West Thirties. Here he entered upon a period of horror. Awaking in the morn and gazing at the hideous wallpaper decorated with enormous red poppies, stained by leaking water pipes, dingy from gas, and marred by match-scratches, he was grudgingly compelled to admit that the Louis family had some merits as interior decorators after all!

His cell would have delighted an entomologist. Various insectivora disported themselves therein, and from time to time an enormous cockroach, who had seen many lodgers come and go, scuttled across the wall, making a dry rustle in its flight.

Long before dawn, the ancient walls shook with the vibration of mighty trucks, and the air quivered with every conceivable squawk, screech, wail, grunt and moan that automobiles can achieve.

By now, Ransom had ceased to haunt the Union, and was asking unblushingly for a job in such quarters as he conceived promising. Nothing came of it. Office staffs were being reduced. Young girls, fresh from night classes, were replacing men. Concerns were not branching out into new fields, but rather retrenching. Capital was wary.

Cassius Breeme, one of Ransom's oldest friends, and by all means the bluntest, summed up the situation, first calling Ezra a blamed fool, and offering to loan him any sum he might name, on his personal note.

"You don't seem to realize," Breeme told him, "that times have changed since you started in for yourself! In those days we used to say that after a young man had saved his first thousand dollars, the worst was over. That's chicken feed today!"

"But you won't deny that I possess some powers of organization?"

"Very true; but nobody is organizing anything! They are hanging on by their eyelids to what they've already got."

"You don't understand, Cassius, that I'm not holding out for a fancy salary! What I'm after is a job. I'm not too proud to accept a sub-ordinate position, at the customary wage. I'm just conceited enough to think I can rise to the top, once I secure an opening. But I've got to have a point of departure!"

"But damn it all, man! What can you do? You couldn't hold down the job of one of my little snub-nosed broilers out there in the office, any more than she could have built up the Ransom Sales Company!"

"What do you mean by that?"

"Well—can you keep books by the Burroughs system? Can you do shorthand? Can you even operate a cash register? Certainly not! Because all these things have been done for you by hirelings; and when you were a clerk, books were kept by a stoop-shouldered man, using a fine pen, and sitting on a high stool; and money was shot into a drawer full of little cup-shaped hollows."

Reluctantly Ransom was obliged to admit the brutal force of

Breeme's arguments. He felt old and tired. For the first time a vague panic stirred in his breast. Incredulously he began to foresee himself in actual want of the bare necessities of life—he who, but a few weeks ago, had donated ten thousand to Bixby for his skill in getting rid of his entire fortune!

Harrowing contingencies pursued themselves through his brain. His bifocal spectacles cost him twenty-five dollars. Suppose he were to break them? One-tenth of his entire fortune would be swept away in one costly tinkle. Why the devil hadn't he bought an extra pair before he wound up his affairs! Once or twice a gold crown had slipped its mooring from a tooth. They cost him a pretty penny to replace. Even so common an emergency as the repairing of his chronometer loomed big in his present condition. With the thought came its corollary—the possible pawning of the watch, if matters did not mend.

All the sordid chain of events which attend the downward steps of the outcast he was experiencing, in the present or in prospect. The sliding down from cheap room to cheaper; the dreary round in search of work; the hunt for inexpensive eating joints; the return on aching feet to a hard bed with none too clean linen.

Finally, unless something broke, the ultimate slump into the cold arms of charity, or the acceptance of loans from old-time business associates, loans that could only postpone the evil day, was the writing on the wall.

Already, though he still carried what would have seemed a fortune to his fellow lodgers, his landlady, with the uncanny prescience of her kind, seemed to him to have sensed his ebbing fortunes. She lurked about his corridor, bobbed up spectrally as he ascended the worn stairs, eyed him with a mournful malevolence. This notwithstanding, he had permitted no hint of shabbiness to appear in his person. His clothes, of plain but expensive material, were unworn; his linen white, his face clean-shaven, his shoes shiny. He was far too intelligent not to realize the subjective and objective disaster certain to follow upon any letting down in his attire or person.

Each week he knocked briskly at the door of his landlady's parlor, and paid her in advance. She accepted with the air of one who counts it a dying effort. The room was funereal to a degree; its heavy marble-topped center-table was cracked through the middle; the "Death of Nelson," and "Napoleon's Grave at St. Helena," stained engravings framed in heavy tarnished gilt; the molting pheasant under its dome, with its one remaining glass-eye bleared and despondent, the black walnut chairs upholstered in faded-red plush—all filled Ransom with a foreboding sense of impending disaster.

There arrived a day when he seriously considered the peddling from door to door of some kitchen utensil or patent gas-tip. Before taking this final plunge into the mercantile depths, he decided to apply at a certain bond-house which, from time to time, employed respectable men to sell small allotments in the tenement districts.

Long since he, who had been carefully guarded in his inner sanctum, had steeled himself against the rebuffs of office boys. Now, with the undying gleam of courage in his eyes, thin shoulders squared, he presented his card to a uniformed young lout, who gazed at it indifferently, then at Ransom curiously, and shuffled off to his superior.

Presently he returned and conducted him to a middle-aged man seated at a desk. He also gazed quizzically from Ransom's card to his face. He was used to this—he knew that he was regarded as a human curiosity; one who had given away a fortune and was now hunting a job.

"You wished, Mr. Ransom?"

"I called to see if you have any present opening for a bond salesman."

The clerk rose to his feet.

"I will take you to our sales manager, Mr. Ransom," he said; and a moment later ushered him into a severely luxurious office. At its flat-topped desk sat a good-looking young man who reached for Ransom's card without looking up, started as if electrified, leaped to his feet, and in one bound reached the old gentleman's side and clasped him in a sinewy embrace.

"Dear old dad!" he cried. "Dapper as ever, on my word! Where on earth have you been hiding, and how did you know I was here?"

Ezra Ransom went limp in his son's arms for the briefest instant, as the discreet clerk tiptoed out and closed the door. But he recovered at once, straightened up, removed and carefully polished his spectacles before replying.

"To be frank about it, Ezra, I didn't! I came here looking for a position. Do you really mean to say you are sales manager here? A concern of this standing!"

"Don't wonder you're stumped, dad! But not half as much as I am to find you actually looking for a job. I pictured you as well on toward your first quarter million before this."

"No, Ezra; I haven't lost my grit, but I've spent my capital—all but about twelve dollars. Your father is an old has-been, Ezra. It cost him a lot of money to find it out!"

"The situation is perfectly logical, dad, when you see it clearly," said the son when he had pulled up a big leather chair for his father and passed him a box of sublimas.

"You see, as the father of your son, you had no standing; but as the son of my father, I had it to burn! You should have seen them tumble over themselves to make a place for Ezra junior! Believe me, I took my pick of a swell lot of offers, and finally came here as a bond salesman.

"I plastered all your old friends and mine with our paper, and when I positively refused to abuse their good nature further, the concern pushed me into this little room as sales manager, and I just bluffed the thing through. Five thousand a year for a starter, and a commission on anything I sell on the side. Not bad—eh?"

Ransom sighed.

"It's what I made my sacrifice to bring to pass, my son. It repays me in full. You're a true Ransom, and you've found yourself! All I ask in return is a small line of securities to market among the little fellows. You seem to have bagged the big game already!"

The son gazed affectionately upon his spruce, indomitable parent, sitting stiff-spined in his easy chair.

"We'll talk that over before a planked steak at the club tonight," he said. "I still belong to two or three of the best ones. And we'll close the office right now. The rest of the day is hereby officially declared to be a legal holiday!"

Hunger

Heritage had passed the stage where he was conscious of hunger. Indeed, there was an almost complete and ascetic severance of mental and physical consciousness, a serene exhilaration in which his mind functioned with amazing clarity.

Questions for whose answer he had often groped blindly were now revealed to him as vividly as a strange countryside is photographed upon the brain at night by a flash of lightning. He did not ponder on futile puzzles whose answer is a matter of numerals or statistical details, but for the first time he was able to grasp the meaning of eternity without beginning or end, of an universe without boundaries. Such a childish device as our Time conception amused him. He perceived the reasonableness of the Fourth Dimension, of other dimensions beyond.

Meanwhile, as he passed through the darkness, it seemed to him that he was immensely tall, his head among the stars, and that instead of walking he remained fixed in space while past him, on either hand, fled the trees and fields, the little hills and the scattered farmsteads. He realized that such a state could not long endure; that his mind was nicely balanced on a thin blade of consciousness from which the slightest breath would overbalance it and plunge him into dark hallucinations. He must eat soon, or delirium would claim him.

It was therefore with a fierce joy that at last, amid all these miles of darkened houses, he beheld a little house whose every window blazed with lights, candle lights; for as he drew near he observed that lighted candles stood in rows on every sill.

Candles are in cathedrals, and coffeehouses. They are lighted in joy and sorrow. They grace austere old houses where are much-worn silver and old books and solid furniture polished by generations of hands, and frowning portraits on faded walls. They burn in thieves' cellars. They are gay, arrogant, furtive. Seen in this isolated house, and

151

long past midnight, they could indicate but one occasion: death!

Heritage, forgetting his first impulse to ask for food, was moved to pause here to pay his respects to the dead. With the urbanity of famine, he would salute the still one, old man, woman, child, with a hail and farewell.

He entered in; and as he thrust open the unlocked door, a venerable man rose and bowed. "I have been waiting," he said simply. "I knew you would come."

"How could you know, when I only took this road, a strange one to me, by chance?"

The old man smiled. "There is no such thing as chance. Of course, I could not know that it would be you, in particular. But someone was bound to come. I need an acolyte, that I may complete my task."

He looked down upon a little trestle-board over which had been thrown a gaudy red tablecloth, and upon which lay a lone roll of fine white linen cloth, like a cocoon, with two large candles burning at each end. The old man, Heritage noted as his eyes became accustomed to the flicker of many little candle flames, wore across his shoulders what appeared to be one of a pair of velour portières, woven with florid designs in red, gold and black. He pointed to the shrouded figure on the trestle-board.

"This is a princess royal," he explained. "Her history is well known to Egyptologists. Because she refused to marry her own brother, her father the pharaoh caused her to be strangled, and her body denied the sacred rites of sepulture. It was embalmed, but thrust into the dry vegetable cellar of a slave's house. I bought it from a great museum of art and antiquities. It took all that I had saved up by fifty years of toil with my pen. Before the Nile grooved its channel to the sea, it was written in the planets that I should perform this thing. But I can not accomplish it alone."

Heritage gravely nodded. "What then can I do?"

The old gentleman handed him two candles, which he had lighted.

"You shall kneel at her feet while I recite the essential part of the ancient rite," he said; and, directly Heritage had knelt, he began rapidly to intone passages from the Book of the Dead.

Tho wavering candlelight served to set everything in the still room into fluidity. The shrouded mummy seemed to breathe rhythmically. In the far corners of the room ludicrous shadows leaped and gamboled. Over Heritage's hands ran little rivulets of hot wax; but he did not feel them, famine having already released him from the tyranny of pain.

Abruptly, the voice of the old man ceased. After a moment he said: "There is no mummy case. That I could not afford to buy. So I have prepared a simple cedar box, lined with soft silk, outside in the grave I have digged for her. And now I must lift her in my arms and take her out; but this is sacrilege, and so, according to the immutable law of old Egypt, you my acolyte must curse me, and make pretense of stoning me."

Heritage bowed. It seemed to him very fitting that he should do these things; and he carefully set down the candles, and took the stone that was handed him.

"May the gods damn your soul for sacrilege," he said, his voice thin and high; and then he feebly cast the stone toward the old man, but not directly at him.

It struck the window at the back of the room; several candles were overturned, and there was a chuckle of glass as one pane was demolished.

From the black night there entered through the broken window-pane two black cats, with jade eyes. With solemn tread, eyes set hard ahead, they passed to the rude trestle, crouched, and leaped upon it, one at the head, the other at the foot, and there began ceremoniously to wash their faces, their soot-black paws making mysterious and cabalistic signs like the passes of a necromancer or the incantations of a priest.

The old man nodded. "It is well," he said; and stooping, lifted the light, dry mummy and bore it from the room and out into the night, followed by the two black cats.

Heritage was left alone with many candles, and the incense smoke from a cracked saucer upon which smoldered strange gums and spices.

Presently, since the old man did not return, he opened the front door and passed through the weed-choked garden and resumed his way down the turnpike, now lighted faintly by the first hint of dawn. By it he perceived that he was come to a covered toll bridge spanning a river. Men had recently been at work restoring its planking; and just as Heritage was about to plunge into the black tunnel, his eyes made out the fragments of a lunch one of the workmen had left behind. There were dry crusts, the fat rind of a slice of ham, a bit of cheese.

With a little sob he sank upon his knees in the wet grass and began to cram the morsels into his avid mouth. And as he swallowed them without chewing, far away across the dark river a cock challenged the dawn.

The Moon-Calves

Perry Hughes occasionally ate in the Getabite cafeteria; but only during the last week of each quarter. From this significant fact, even Dr. Watson would readily have deduced that he was a remittance man, and the Getabite cashier was a far keener observer than the satellite of Sherlock Holmes. She knew a surprising lot about the cafeteria patrons. Her final judgment of them was formed after she had learned just what classes they did or did not belong in.

For instance, Hughes belonged to that very limited cafeteria group which eats its eggs from the shell. And he did it deftly, and without self-consciousness. Next, he belonged to another small unit whose members prop reading matter against the sugar bowl while eating. The cashier did not count newspapers; she meant what she termed "lit'rachoor." To the much larger group which helped itself from the toothpick bowl on the cigar case, Mr. Hughes did not belong.

Her knowledge was even more specific. She knew his name, having seen it stamped in gold on his pigskin billfold when he paid his check; and the distended condition of the wallet, with the very few greenbacks it held, indicated infallibly that he had it in bales, but was now up against it.

In one respect alone he did not classify at all. He was sui generis. To the cashier's positive knowledge, he was the only male patron of the Getabite who could not have told the color of her hair or eyes. He apparently looked upon her as one does on a nickel-in-the-slot machine. She had purposely delayed in handing back his change, and he had merely glanced up in a bored way, as one does if a slab of chewing gum or box of matches does not instantly materialize when one drops a coin into the proper slot.

She had even spoken to him. Nothing fresh, of course. Tessie Desmond was not that kind of a girl! But she had said, "Thank you, Mr. Hughes!" once or twice when he paid, and he had not seemed gratified or even surprised that she knew his name. Probably he took it quite for granted that everybody knew it. Conceited puppy!

Even as the words formed in her mind, she was honest enough to repudiate them. He wasn't that. No one could be less self-conscious, more abstracted than this quietly yet "swell" dressed young man of thirty, with rather sad, twinkling brown eyes, if you get the idea. It wasn't conceivable that he was a hermit; but she had to confess that he might as well be, so far as she was concerned.

There is an excellent plating which looks more like refined gold than gold itself does, just as there are wax flowers more perfect than nature can produce, and extemporaneous hair which is blonder than anything in Scandinavia. Tessie was a natural blonde; hence her tresses held glints of amber and red as the light, sun or arc, played over it, and her brows were darker instead of being perfectly matched as they would have been in any beauty shop. There was mingled gold and black in her eyes, and a dimple at the right of her red, smiling lips was cunningly balanced by a faint freckle on the left of her short nose.

Eighteen, slender but well-rounded, and breathing such perfection of health and vitality that one sensed at once a clean, if not aristocratic ancestry, Tessie's instinctive taste led her to follow the prevailing mode of dress with reservations. She wore her heels and skirt at least two inches lower than her more extreme friends did, and she refused to roll her near-silk stockings; and nearly half of her pretty, close-set ears were visible, unless her hair became unruly.

She felt certain that Mr. Perry Hughes would feel repaid could she but once manage to catch his eyes. In the end, it was a profound sigh which attracted his attention. Glancing up, he beheld all that has been detailed, with every feature and attitude denoting extreme dejection.

"What seems to be the trouble?" he asked.

He had a nice voice; virile, but low-pitched, and with what Tessie, with memories of stock-company Britons, would have called an English accent; but which was really Harvard grafted on to West Pennsylvanian.

"It's thinkin' about that gold tooth I gotta have put in," she sighed.

The young man regarded her parted lips, disclosing teeth as nearly perfect as anything except an artificial set can be.

"I can't imagine such a necessity," he commented, his eyes straying from her mouth to other delectable features. He was conscious of a faint surprise that he had not noticed her before.

"Oh, it ain't *necess'ry*," Tessie reassured him. "But all my friends have got a gold tooth! They tell me mine look kinda monotonous; that a gold one would go well with my hair an' eyes."

"Oh, I say! That would be a terrible pity," Perry Hughes protested. "I have a gold crown, but am thankful to say it is back out of sight on a wisdom tooth. Nothing would tempt me to have one in front."

The cashier wriggled contentedly on her high seat. The conversation was pleasantly personal and informal.

"Do you honestly wish I wouldn't, then?" she speculated, tilting back her head and regarding him thoughtfully through narrowed lids.

The occasional patron of the Getabite looked both puzzled and amused.

"Why, I should hardly consider it to be any of my business!"

"Oh, I don't feel that way, Mr. Hughes, a-tall! I know you have good taste."

"I don't see how you know anything of the sort."

"I've seen you eat eggs," she candidly explained. "An' other things about you. I guess I'm a quick study, sorta."

He felt that the situation was rather getting out of his hands, and stalled by purchasing a brand of cigarettes he would never dream of smoking. He even lighted one. This seemed to restore his aplomb. It was probably why actors always did it in the mimic crises of the stage. He turned as he was passing out, and touched his hat brim.

"Think it over a day or so, at least," he urged.

As a matter of fact, his quarterly check was due today, and he had anticipated several weeks of real dining before the wolf chased him into the Getabite again.

II.

Perry Hughes, Sr., had sold out his little foundry to a syndicate, they had gouged him pretty deep. He never contrived to get back on his feet again, and although all during young Perry's Harvard days the motherless household was maintained on a rather lavish scale, there wasn't much left when the old gentleman suddenly died. He had regarded his son's business instinct with deep abhorrence, and had frankly told him that he was atavistic; a throwback, or "sport," on the family tree, which, through many generations of handpicked marriages, had become anemic.

"There's nothing positively bad about you," Perry remembered hearing him state, not a month prior to his death. "Sometimes I wish there was! I don't know anything that will save you except to marry some intelligent country cook who never smelled gasoline or sat up later than nine o'clock in her life!"

Things went well enough, on the whole. The only trouble was, there was just one week too many in each month, Perry decided. His allowance was ample for three weeks, but not for four. That was why he ate at the Getabite, as Tessie Desmond had easily guessed. There were much better cafeterias; but Perry's sole idea was to pacify his hunger as cheaply as possible, and he had wandered into the Getabite by chance, and gone back to it by habit. He read while eating, to forget where he was.

He belonged to two good clubs, and lived in one of them; but he was apt to be posted for dues there, and no food was served at the other. As he left the Getabite after his first chat with its cashier, he planned to go at once upon receipt of his quarterly check, cash it at the club and pay up his dues, and dine luxuriously that evening. He did, in fact, get his name removed from the delinquent list, but most surprisingly, with the pigskin billfold stuffed full once more, he found himself heading, at six o'clock, for the cafeteria.

Tessie had thought much and tenderly about him during the afternoon. Like himself, she was an orphan; but she had no family tree. This was not because there had been anything to conceal in the lives of her ancestors, but that there had been little to record. She knew that the first Desmond had been a Huguenot refugee, who settled in Delaware, where the family had always lived. Her father, employed in a munitions factory, had risen high — along with a ton or so of T. N. T. — and much of him had never come down. At least, they never found much. Then her mother had married a market gardener, and Tessie's youth was spent in going to a village school, and weeding onions and transplanting lettuce during vacations. Stepbrothers and stepsisters came, and Tessie's mother died. She found herself edged out of the nest, and fluttered to New York.

In time the tan and calluses of the outdoor life wore off, and all but one of the freckles. There remained an exuberant vitality, and a prettiness notable even on Broadway. Several times she had been obliged to resign because of temperamental employers. On such occasions her sharp tongue reduced their stature by at least a cubit. She always found it easy to get a new place. Her present one was untroubled, since the owner of the Getabite was a middle-aged failure without ambition or vices.

III.

Tessie was just leaving the cafeteria as Perry Hughes arrived. It was her short day, when she was on duty from noon until six. On alternate days she worked until noon, returning at six to remain until midnight. Lomasney, the owner, alternated with her, and had just seated himself beside the cash register as the girl, attractive in blue tricotine and darker blue straw toque, passed out to the street.

Hughes paused on seeing her. He knew nothing about her hours; had not thought of them. His return to the Getabite on this night, when he might have eaten wherever he chose, had been solely on her account. All the afternoon her gold-black eyes had followed him, and her ridiculous notion about a gold tooth had caused him many smiles. He had made no plans for improving the acquaintance; nothing beyond securing a table from which he could observe her, and see if she really was as distractingly pretty as she had seemed.

Now, seeing her on the point of leaving, he stopped uncertainly, not wishing to have her see him turn away for no reason, but unable to think of anything to say.

Tessie, who knew perfectly well why he hesitated, took matters in her own hands in order to give him time to collect himself. It was highly gratifying to her to know that he did not care to go inside now that she was off duty; and as it was evident that he must go somewhere, and the same was true for herself, it was possible that, with a little encouragement, he might ask her to dine with him, and perhaps go to a movie later.

This was not at all her custom. She sometimes went with a party to dinner, and now and then to the pictures with some nice boy; but not to dinner with him. There was a young Greek who kept a fruit store near the Getabite — a suave, black-eyed man of uncertain temper, who had pestered her for the past six months with all sorts of invitations; but Tessie did not like him, and resented his fits of jealousy. But she knew that if Perry were to invite her, she would go anywhere he suggested; and she stopped and spoke to him, to give him time to feel at ease. It would have amused the sophisticated Perry to know that a little nobody like Tessie felt that he must be put at his ease.

She smiled at him and said: "The goulash and noodles is good tonight, if you're real hungry. But lay off the Irish stew; not enough Irish in it!"

Perry smiled back at her.

"You're not going for that gold tooth, are you, Miss — er —"

"Desmond. *Tessie.* No — I'm going to put my own teeth into something hearty. I can't eat in a place I work in, after smelling the cooking all day!"

"I'm not keen about goulash and noodles," confided Perry.

Tessie waited, calmly surveying the throng of clerks and stenographers, and bobbing her pert turban in greeting from time to time. She was in no hurry; there was nothing to do till tomorrow.

"I say — why not come and have dinner with me?"

The man looked anxiously at her unconcerned and very perfect profile. "We've both got to eat. Why not together?"

She turned slowly toward him, her long lashes masking the triumph in her gold-black eyes.

"Uh-huh. Sure! We'll make it Dutch."

"We'll do nothing of the sort, I have oodles of money tonight. We'll eat in a regular place — not meaning to knock the Getabite!"

"O-oh!" She prolonged the vowel, and her gaze. "Then your allowance came today?"

His own eyes widened.

"How did you — what do you mean?"

Tessie laughed. She had a nice, gurgly laugh that began deep in her round white throat, and it ended by a thrust of the extreme tip of her tongue between her teeth.

"Why else would you eat at our place on the last few days of the quarter, and no other times? Don't you s'pose I been broke, too? Only with me it's at the end of the week, instead of the quarter."

"You're a regular little sleuth! That reminds me that you know my name, too, though I do not recall mentioning it, or signing I.O.U.'s at the Getabite? Just how much do you know about me, anyhow?"

"Enough so I'm accepting an invitation to dinner, Mr. Hughes."

"Then you don't know the worst, for which I'm grateful. Haven't you a coat or something, to wear over that thin suit?"

"Sounds like Coney," she speculated.

"But isn't. Not with me! We're going to fly high tonight."

She nodded, and darted back into the cafeteria to take a blue cloak which hung on its hook back of her cage.

"Whassa matter?" the despondent Lomasney asked, looking up from his nearly empty cash register. "Change in the weather?"

"I'm elopin'," she flung back at him with a smile.

"I'll be doin' it all by myself, if business falls off much more!" Lomasney grumbled.

Perry threw her cloak over his arm, and signaled a passing taxi.

"To the Moon-Fixers!" he said to the chauffeur.

"Where's that?" Tessie queried, wrinkling her nose.

"To tell the truth, I've never been there; but some of my friends have. It's the latest jazzery, and about the most expensive. I feel in the mood for it tonight."

It was a good ten-mile drive up the Hudson before their car drew up at the end of an already fairly long line of waiting taxis and roadsters. They alighted, and walked a short distance beside a high brick wall to a wide entrance beyond which was a roomy lawn dotted with elms, from whose boughs Japanese lanterns cast a varicolored glow over many little tables gleaming with linen and cut glass and silver. Behind a syringa a Filipino orchestra drowned out the more musical katydids and crickets.

A dancing pavilion bounded the lawn at one side, and its far end overlooked the Hudson, a silver roadstead in the moonlight. But there was nothing in all this to distinguish the place from dozens of other roadhouses. What set the Moon-Fixers apart, and gave it its name, was a novelty in the presence of half a dozen captive balloons, tethered to earth by a stout hempen cable wound on a drum. In each basket, which was reached by a short rope ladder, was a little *table à deux*. The successive courses were sent up in a wicker service container; and the couverte charge for the privilege of dining above the earth was twenty-five dollars.

It was toward one of these swaying monsters that Perry guided his pop-eyed little companion.

A waiter wound up the drum, and the basket slowly descended until its rope ladder touched the dew-drenched lawn. Tessie nimbly clambered up and inside, with a whip of skirts and a flash of silken ankles. Perry followed, and seated himself across the diminutive table from her in one of the two wicker chairs. There wasn't a foot of space to spare.

The waiter scribbled the order on his pad, and placed olives and salted almonds and celery hearts on the table. Then he began to unwind the drum, and foot by foot they rose, level with the swinging Japanese lanterns, up among the elm boughs, clearing their tops, to come to rest gently swaying a hundred feet in the air.

Directly below them, the lanterns formed a misty screen of colored light through which rose the softened wails of ukulele and steel guitar, the laughter and chatter of those dining al fresco on the lawn, the shuffle of pumps on the pavilion floor. As they were the first to dine in the air tonight, they were as much alone as if they had taken refuge in the fourth dimension. Far below, and a little to one side, the Hudson lay in a ribbon of dull silver, the mists clinging to its surface.

Tessie sighed.

"I'll say we're on the top of the world!" she declared. "I don't believe there is any such place as we're in. Don't wake me up!"

"Thought you'd like it," Perry nodded at her. "Pretty clever idea somebody had, what?"

A buzzer sounded beneath the table, and there appeared at the outer rim of their basket a little cage containing their oysters. Perry removed them, touched the button which sounded another buzzer down below, and the container descended.

There was quite a little air stirring, and the two-inch guardrail on the table was needed to keep the dishes out of their laps. A great tureen of *purée Mongols* followed their oysters; a sizzling hot lake trout came next. The cool night air whipped their healthy young appetites; and for a space they devoted themselves to the dinner, speaking only in fragments.

By the time they had finished the trout, another balloon joined them, just far enough away to avoid danger of collision. They exchanged jovial greetings with the intruders, a fat, bald gentleman, rather nervous, and a slim girl ostentatiously at ease.

"I knew you were worth knowing," said Tessie as her host served a ruddy cut of beef a full inch thick. "But I certainly thought you'd never sit up and take notice!"

"You brought me to life with that awful gold tooth idea. Hope you have changed your mind?"

"Well — I had to do *something* to get you to talk!"

"You mean you were not in earnest?"

"Who — me? Not so you'd notice it! I just made that up as I went along."

Perry grinned.

"I fell for it all right! But why I never noticed you before I can't imagine. Suppose it was because I was always broke, and low-spirited when I went to the Getabite. Used to wish I could sleep through the last week of the quarter."

"I know the feeling," Tessie nodded. "But at least you didn't have to work. It's bad enough to have to eat at the Getabite — let alone work there!"

He patted the firm little hand that held her water glass. She looked reflectively at it, but made no move to withdraw it.

"Seems to me you don't show much business sense, Mr. Hughes."

"Please say Perry — at least, till we get back to earth!"

"Well, then, Perry, I don't know what it costs to eat in a balloon, but I can see you hitting a one-arm chair more'n a week to pay for this spree."

"Righto. But isn't it worth it? You are not the first to observe that I am no young Napoleon of finance. That's why my dad left everything in trust. Trouble is, there are too many weeks in a month. If there were only three, I'd live like a lord!"

Tessie shook her head vigorously.

"No, you wouldn't. You'd spend twice as much in the first two weeks, and go broke the third. And if you got your income once a year, you'd starve along about November."

Perry for the third time sounded the buzzer on the table.

"That waiter must have forgotten he has a party in the sky," he grumbled.

"There's a lot of this dinner coming yet — and it's getting cool up here."

He leaned over the basket edge and peered down through the darkness, shading his eyes from the electric candelabra over their table.

Then, an astounding thing happened. Japanese lanterns, elm trees, all the dimly visible earth seemed to drop away from them, leaving them resting in space.

Tessie saw things differently. She was looking idly at the couple fifty feet away, and as usual with her, placing them in their proper classes. Suddenly she shot above them. She had the briefest glimpse of the fat man's face, mouth open, and a large portion of sweetbread arrested on its journey. She heard the shrill diminuendo of the girl's scream, noticed that the Filipino band seemed to die away to the mere ghost of syncopated melody. She leaned across the table and seized Perry's arm.

"We're off!" she shouted to him. "Our balloon's broke away, and we're going up a mile a minute!"

IV.

From his fruit store two doors below the Getabite, Demetrius Pappas had beheld with deep resentment the encounter of Tessie and her young "gentleman friend."

He was a passionate man, with a glossy black mustache and a jealous nature. Often he had tried to induce the pretty cashier to dine with him at the Marathon or Minerva coffee house; and she had always replied that while she might go with a feller to a picture, maybe, that was her limit. Now, observing intelligently that the man with whom she was talking was far above him in class, a gentleman and presumably rich, he knew that at this hour she would be going out to eat; and he watched them narrowly to see what might happen.

When the girl re-entered the cafeteria to appear an instant later with her cloak, while her companion signaled a taxi, Demetrius suspected the very worst. He edged up to them, mingling with the six o'clock throng, and for once the sharp-eyed Tessie, absorbed in her conquest, failed to notice his proximity. So it was that he heard his rival direct the chauffeur to drive to the Moon-Fixers' restaurant.

He had never heard of this place; but he found it listed in the telephone directory. He slipped a sharp banana knife with an ugly curved blade in his pocket, left his fruit stall in charge of his assistant, and set out to follow. He had no definite plan in mind. He was given to brief fits of violent rage, although in general a sunny child of the Levant.

He did nothing so foolishly extravagant as to hire a taxi; but having learned where the Moon-Fixers was, he was able to get a surface car for nearly half the distance, and set out to walk the rest of the way. He argued that his prey would spend a couple of hours, at least, over their dinner, and that there would be plenty of time.

On arriving, he strolled about the grounds, observing each table, looking on at the dancers in the pavilion, making a careful survey of the entire place. He had about made up his mind they were not there, when his sharp ears detected Tessie's laughter floating down from somewhere above the Japanese lanterns.

When he had satisfied himself that the two were alone in the balloon, far above him and out of reach, his rage, which had been gradually cooling in the night air, flared up afresh. He observed the waiter sending up expensive food by a pulley, heard above the whining of the Filipino orchestra snatches of laughter and talk from the gently swaying basket above the tree-tops.

While the waiter was engaged in seating some fresh arrivals, Demetrius Pappas edged up to the wooden drum, to which was attached the cable. It was now quite dark, and nobody paid any attention to him. There were many, singly and in pairs, strolling about the spacious grounds.

It was but the work of a second to whip out the banana knife, and with one slashing stroke, sever the hempen cable. An instant later Demetrius had slipped around an elm tree, crossed over to the pavilion, and passed out through the entrance just as the place began to hum with the news that one of the captive balloons had worked loose with a party of diners.

There was, in fact, more excitement among those left behind on earth than in the runaway balloon itself. The great bag shot straight up at first, but the occupants of the basket were not conscious of any violent motion. Low-hanging clouds hovered over the valley of the Hudson,

and in a few moments they passed through these and found themselves
bathed in moonlight. The balloon ceased to rise, and, borne along by a
steady easterly breeze, it swept over the fleecy cloud floor, across which
their black shadow pursued them. Overhead fled the golden phalanx of
the stars, while the full moon, seeming to have doubled in size, raced
with them in playful rivalry.

The two refugees were still seated. There was no room to move
about. They clasped hands, straining toward one another across the
table.

"It's incredible that such a thing could happen, but it has," said
Perry, his voice sounding hollow in the great void. "Your people — they
will never forgive me —"

Her fingers moved ever so slightly in his.

"I have none."

"There must be *somebody* who cares?"

"Old Lomasney will be peeved if I'm not in my cage at six sharp.
There's nobody who counts. No one I'd rather be alone with up here
than you!"

He tightened his grip on her little hands.

"And you're not afraid?"

"I don't think so. Somehow, looking at this" — she lifted her face
to the moon-shot sky — "we seem sort of unimportant. Awful small, if
you get the idea."

He inclined his head in sympathetic understanding. Below them
the clouds lay as solid as a sea. One might conceivably drown in them;
but it seemed impossible that one could fall through to the vanished
earth beneath. Here and there were rents, like deep wells at the bottom
of which glimmered faint lights, representing sleeping towns over
which they were drifting.

Tessie shivered a little, and released one hand to draw closer about
her neck a small fur piece.

"That's effective," approved Perry, seeking to distract her mind by
compliment.

"Huh!" She scorned. "Monkey fur."

"And isn't that worn this season?" He laughed.

"I s'pose it is — by monkeys! But not by regular folks. It's all the fur I got. Which goes for monkeys, too."

Before they realized that they were descending, they found themselves smothered in cold, clammy mist. Then the earth burst into view, a patchwork of moonlighted spaces spangled on ink-black shadows.

"A lot depends on where we land," Perry worried, "I believe balloonists toss overboard one of their fifty-pound bags of sand when they want to rise."

He had a vague notion that these bags were heaved over bodily — not realizing the effect this would have on whomever a fifty-pound sand bag might drop from a distance of a mile or so!

"Hold tight to the ropes," he warned, and held her shoulders until she did so. "I'll try tossing over the table. It's in the way, anyhow. Here goes!"

First the dishes, then the table itself. So rapid was their own descent that at first the table seemed to hang suspended in air beside them. Then, as they leaped upward, it shot out of sight.

They now sat down in the basket, peering over the rim. They did not again pierce the cloud belt; and as no broad fields suitable for a landing appeared below, and after a time they began to descend once more, the chairs were thrown over.

By good luck no one was injured. It was very late — long past midnight — and few were astir in the rural section over which they were passing. An Italian truck gardener was amazed the following morning to discover a perfectly good set of tableware, each piece bearing an embossed half moon, in his onion field. As there were no footprints anywhere about save his own, it was manifestly a miracle. A mile away a farmer speculated on the strange vision of a wrecked table lodged on the ridgepole of his barn; but by noon the story of the runaway balloon had spread over the country.

For a long time after discarding the chairs, the derelict swept steadily south and east, very gradually sinking earthward, until Perry became alarmed as the tallest trees thrust upward at them with menacing boughs. There was nothing more to throw overboard, and it was evident that before long they would make a forced landing.

"Ought to be a rip-cord, somewhere; but I don't see any. Just as well, perhaps. I might let out all the gas at once, and drop us like a sinker," he thought.

Once they swung perilously near a white village steeple, just as its solemn bell struck the hour of two. Twice they missed a hillock by yards; and for a long time they skimmed along a marsh, from which millions of frogs jeered at them.

Perry reached out and gathered Tessie into his arms in the shelter of their basket. She snuggled warm and fragrant there, her head against his breast. Presently her own arms stole up and about his neck, and her lips were on his. Traveling with the wind, there was no sense of motion, no discomforting breeze. They seemed suspended in a golden flood of moonshine. It was as if they were alone in the firmament, companions of the planets, and floating in the midst of dead worlds.

He was the first to recall their peril. Glancing over the basket edge he was horrified to see that they were a scant ten feet above ground, and hurtling toward a row of long, narrow white buildings.

"Hold tight!" he bawled, wrenching her arms from his neck, and guiding her hands to the supporting ropes. "Don't jump, whatever happens!"

Hardly were the words spoken than with a shock like the end of the world, their basket struck. As they were hurled out, there came a ripping crash, and in an instant they were in the midst of a multitude of fluffy white, flapping, and frantically squawking creatures. Then, with a spine-jarring bump, they sat on Mother Earth.

Minds and bodies were stunned for the moment. They were roused by the sound of voices, and the winking of lanterns.

"Head the varmints off, Jawn! We'll try what a load of double-B'll do to the pesky hen thieves!"

The lights separated, and heavy footfalls became audible. Perry rose unsteadily to his feet. He cautiously raised Tessie.

"Anything broken?" he whispered.

"Everything, I guess! But I don't seem to mind it."

"We must have lighted in a chicken-run; let's go while the going's good."

At this instant an amazed cry startlingly near at hand arrested them.

"Pa! Looka here! They've gone an' ripped off the hull roof of the white Orpingtons' roost!"

A deeper voice answered from somewhere to the left:

"They couldn't! There wasn't time. It'd take a couple o' hours to do that."

"You just come an' see for yerself! I tell ye they *hev*!"

A consultation followed, and the trespassers took advantage of it to steal away. They fetched up several times against chicken wire, and disturbed numbers of outraged Orpingtons rendered homeless by the sudden snatching away of their rooftree; but at length they found a gate, and slipped through, and across a field to a well-traveled road.

Their balloon, lightened of its passengers, had leaped high in air, and was doubtless several miles away by now.

"Here's where we count the ties back to Broadway," sighed Tessie. "The show's over."

She smiled up at him, and put her hand in his. They swung gaily up the white highway, not much caring where they were.

"This road must lead somewhere, and I've the price of gasoline!" Perry declared. "We'll breakfast in town yet."

In fact, a scant mile brought them to a sizable village, and at its garage they awakened a night man, and learned that they were in Long Island.

"Broke down a mile back, and want to get carried to New York," Perry explained.

The man rubbed his eyes and grumbled. Although his sole reasons for staying at the garage nights was to profit by just such mishaps, he seemed sore at having his nap spoiled.

"'S a long ways. Cost ya twenty," he said.

Perry promptly peeled off a couple of tens and offered them.

"Hurry up, then!"

The car was rather shabby, but in good condition; and shortly they were speeding toward home.

"No more work at the cafeteria, Tessie," said Perry Hughes, drawing her close to him in the darkened rear seat.

"How do you get that way? We're back on earth now — not up in the clouds with the moon!"

"I'm serious! I don't want anything in the world but you, now. The license and the ring are my first errands after we have some coffee."

Tessie laughed contentedly.

"It listens pretty in the moonlight," she admitted. "But how about that last week in the quarter? You can't stretch your income for one, now. It'd crack, trying to feed two. Wait!" As he started to protest, "I got a lot better plan than that. My boss is all ready to quit cold. He's got a three-year lease, and a trade that's falling off every day. Why? Because he's a simp! The Getabite oughta show a clear profit of twenty beans a day. It did once. But he's got no sense. Hires a chef that can't cook fish decent — and blooey! Goes our whole Friday business. Skimps his coffee four ounces to the gallon, and it tastes like tea. Boils his tea, and it tastes like coffee. Nothing served warm — except the ice water."

"Well — what of it? What's it all to me? I don't intend to eat there after you are Mrs. Hughes!"

"You don't have to; but if you will show a little courage I'll make you like it! And bring your friends, too. As I say, the old man is all in. He'd jump at any kind of an offer. A thousand dollars would buy the Getabite. Say three hundred down, and give my boss notes for the rest. Couldn't you fix that?"

"Why, yes; I suppose so. I could even pay that much cash. Of course! But what do I want of a cafeteria?"

"Ain't I telling you? So's you can have twenty a day to add to what you got — and a place to eat in for nothing the last week of each quarter! And speakin' for myself, so's the future Mrs. Hughes can buy herself a trousseau befittin' her silk-stocking fiancé!"

It took quite a bit of argument to convince Perry, but he had capitulated before Brooklyn was reached.

"It's horrible to think of having you go to work after such a night, without one wink of sleep!"

"Never you mind me; reading the newspaper accounts of the missing balloon, and making change at the same time, will keep me awake till noon. Then the hay, till six. My bad time will come between ten and twelve tonight."

"I'll be there to stay awake with you," he promised.

"We'll drink black coffee and yawn in each other's faces," she prophesied.

It was quarter to six o'clock when the shabby car was dismissed a few blocks from the Getabite.

Perry bought an armful of morning papers, the headlines of each featuring their mishap and hinting at the worst.

"I'll never go back to pay that dinner check," he said. "Their own fault. Could sue them if it wasn't for the notoriety. Must find out who that chicken-breeder was, though, and send him a bank note."

Considering their thrilling night, they parted in very matter-of-fact manner. It wasn't Perry's fault. The street was too crowded.

Tessie, looking as fresh as if she had had a ten-hour sleep, tripped into her cage five minutes ahead of time. Perry turned toward his club. He yawned and passed a hand over his chin. It rasped sharply.

"I need a shave and bath, and a lot of coffee, and a sleep," he reflected. "Outside of kiting all over Long Island and ruining a perfectly good hen house, and agreeing to buy a cafeteria, and getting myself engaged to the greatest little pal in the world, I spent a quiet evening!"

Demetrius Pappas watched him go.

His fit of jealous rage had passed quickly, and all night he had sat in the Minerva Cafe, consuming endless cups of syrupy-black coffee. He was filled with remorse, and dreaded to look at the early papers lest he read news that would convict him, in his soul, as a murderer.

He beheld the arrival of the two at six o'clock, afoot, and unconcerned. His simple soul was puzzled, but vastly relieved. He turned to an early customer, and with a clean sweep of his knife — the selfsame one that had severed the balloon cable — he removed six nice yellow bananas from the parent stalk.

"Fif-a-teen cent!"

He smiled and forgot all about his blighted affections.

www.ingramcontent.com/pod-product-compliance
Lightning Source LLC
Chambersburg PA
CBHW050746250626
47155CB00005B/1944